April 1982

Give a Corpse a Bad Name

When Elizabeth Ferrars turned to writing crime novels she had been living for some time in Devonshire. Not surprisingly, therefore, *Give a Corpse a Bad Name*, first published in 1940, was set in the Devon countryside, because she has always attached great importance to the accurate and well-realized settings, mostly domestic, for which she has become famous.

She has usually dispensed with a series detective, but her first five novels all featured a character named Toby Dyke, an ex-reporter, now of no fixed occupation. It is Toby who, in conjunction with the local police, investigates the curious circumstances attending the death of a middle-aged stranger who is run over by a car one winter's night while lying dead drunk in the middle of a Devon lane. Driving the car is Anna Milne, an attractive widow from South Africa. By chance (is it?) the dead man also comes from South Africa. And he has Anna Milne's address in his pocket . . .

Toby claims to live by his wits, and there is plenty for him and his friend George to set those wits to work on, for even in her first novel, the plot which Elizabeth Ferrars unfolds has the deceptively simple complexity which her readers have come to expect.

by the same author

EXPERIMENT WITH DEATH
DESIGNS ON LIFE
WITNESS BEFORE THE FACT
IN AT THE KILL
LAST WILL AND TESTAMENT
MURDERS ANONYMOUS
THE PRETTY PINK SHROUD
BLOOD FLIES UPWARDS
THE CUP AND THE LIP
DROWNED RAT
ALIVE AND DEAD
HANGED MAN'S HOUSE
THE SMALL WORLD OF MURDER
FOOT IN THE GRAVE
BREATH OF SUSPICION
A STRANGER AND AFRAID
SKELETON STAFF
THE SEVEN SLEEPERS
THE SWAYING PILLARS
NO PEACE FOR THE WICKED
ZERO AT THE BONE
NINTH LIFE
A LEGAL FICTION
THE DOUBLY DEAD
THE WANDERING WIDOWS
THE BUSY BODY
THE SLEEPING DOGS
FEAR THE LIGHT
ENOUGH TO KILL A HORSE
ETC., ETC.

ELIZABETH FERRARS

Give a Corpse a Bad Name

A FAMOUS FIRST

COLLINS, ST JAMES'S PLACE, LONDON

William Collins Sons & Co. Ltd.
London · Glasgow · Sydney · Auckland
Toronto · Johannesburg

First published 1940
Reprinted in this edition 1981

ISBN 0 00 231294 8

Photoset in Compugraphic Baskerville
Printed in Great Britain by
T. J. Press (Padstow) Ltd

The characters in this book are entirely imaginary
and have no relation to any living persons

CHAPTER 1

At six-thirty on a Tuesday evening near the beginning of January Anna Milne was heard by her parlourmaid to say: 'Damn the man, he's late!'

At six-forty-five the girl, returning from the errand that had taken her past the open door of the drawing-room, overheard the words: 'To hell with him, I can't wait!'

Three minutes later she saw Mrs Milne come out of the drawing-room, pick up the fur coat that had been thrown down on a chair, put it on over the white skirt and knitted jumper she was wearing, pick up the badminton racket leaning against the chair, and go out by the front door.

At six-fifty the lights of Mrs Milne's Bentley flickered past the windows of the house. The parlour-maid, returning to the kitchen, told the cook what she had heard.

Until past seven o'clock they discussed the language often used by Mrs Milne. They disapproved of it.

At twenty minutes after midnight a white-faced woman in a fur coat walked into the police station in the village of Chovey.

She entered and crossed so swiftly to where the constable on duty was re-reading the racing news in the local evening paper that although he recognized her he had no time to rise to his feet.

She grasped the edge of the desk before him, put her face close to his, and said: 'Smell my breath. Am I drunk?'

Startled, the constable sniffed.

'One beer,' she said, 'more than an hour ago.'

'Yes, ma'am, that seems about right.'

'Then for God's sake,' she said, dropping into the nearest chair, 'get me a drink. I need one.'

The constable got it.

'There's a nasty mess up the road,' said Mrs Milne. 'I've run over a man and killed him. You'd better come along.'

CHAPTER 2

Mrs Milne was a widow in her early forties. Five years ago she and her daughter Daphne had come to live in Chovey. She was of medium height, lightly and strongly built, with dark hair and dark eyes, deep-set, and strongly defined features. Her coat was of mink—expensive.

The police whisky steadied her nerves and brought a spot of red to each of her cheek-bones.

To Sergeant Eggbear, summoned by Constable Leat, she gave the details of the accident.

'It's between the two bridges on the Purbrook road—you know where I mean? Those two hump-backed bridges. He was lying across the road—dead drunk, I suppose. I didn't knock him down. I never saw anything. I was a bit dazzled by a car that passed the other way and didn't dip its lights. I'd drawn in to the side to let it pass just before the first of the bridges, then when it had come over and gone by I went over myself, and about half-way between the bridges I felt a jolt . . .'

'I been expectin' somethin' o' the sort ever since I come here,' said the sergeant.

'Aye, they'm dangerous, they bridges,' said Leat, 'and yet 'tis the first accident us've 'ad there.'

'Could you say just about what time it happened, ma'am?' said the sergeant.

Anna Milne rubbed a knuckle against her forehead in a

nervous gesture. There was a blankness in her eyes almost as if she had not comprehended the question. She answered jerkily, 'About midnight, was it?'

' 'Twas twelve-thirty when the lady come into the station,' said Leat.

'About midnight,' Mrs Milne repeated. She had a quiet but rather rough voice. 'Yes, something like that. I'd been in Purbrook, playing badminton at the Red Dragon, and I gave some people a lift home. Miss Willis —d'you know her? She lives a little way down the main Plymouth road. I took her home. But I dropped Major Maxwell first. His car was out of order and I'd picked him up earlier and promised to drive him home again. I dropped him at the crossroads and then turned down to the left to drop Miss Willis—'

'Then you turned back and come back to the crossroads?' said the sergeant.

'Yes, and came on home. It must have been about midnight that it happened.'

'And you say that you didn't see the—um, man?' said the sergeant.

'No,' said Mrs Milne.

'Not even a dark shape like, lying in the road?'

'No!' she repeated vehemently, 'I saw nothing—nothing at all! I only felt . . .'

'There, there, ma'am,' said the sergeant automatically, and licked the tip of his pencil. 'If you would just describe what you did on realizing that a tragedy had taken place . . .'

An odd, brilliant smile tightened the slack muscles of her face. 'A tragedy, sergeant? You're jumping to conclusions. I haven't told you who the man is.'

The sergeant's gaze jerked up from his note-book. 'I understood, from the way you began your story, ma'am, that you didn't know yourself.'

'I don't,' said Anna Milne.

'Then—'

'So perhaps it's not a tragedy after all. You can't tell, can you? Perhaps I've killed someone who needed killing, or someone who'll be happier dead. Perhaps I haven't robbed any home of a breadwinner, or any woman of her lover, or even posterity of a remarkable genius, or—'

'Here, ma'am,' said Leat, 'have another drop of this.'

'Thank you,' said Anna Milne.

There was a silence while she gulped down the whisky and, for a moment, sat breathing fast, her eyes looking glassily past the sergeant at a calendar on the wall. Then she asked if she might smoke. Before she received any answer she had stuck a cigarette in her mouth. But her lighter, as she flicked at the little wheel, sparked only faintly and did not catch alight. Holding it in one hand she took the cigarette from her lips and said in an even tone: 'Once when I was broke I went round betting half a crown with anyone who'd take it on that their lighter wouldn't work the first time. I made twenty-seven and six the first week and lived on it for a fortnight. You understand, sergeant, this is absolutely the first time a thing like this has happened to me. I've run over a dog, and I've wrung the necks of a good many chickens in cold blood, but this is positively my first experience of killing a man.'

'Maybe you didn't kill'n, ma'am,' said the sergeant.

'What?' she said. 'D'you think he could have been dead already? Will you be able to tell?'

'Maybe he ain't dead.'

Mrs Milne jumped to her feet. 'You think I'd let you sit here wasting time if—?'

'That's all right, ma'am,' said the sergeant, 'I sent the ambulance around first thing. But I thought it'd give you a little time to recover yourself if I questioned you here before we set off for the scene of the accident.'

'I'm a fool,' said Mrs Milne dryly. She sat down. 'But he's dead all right. I know the dead when I meet them.'

'Perhaps if you would just tell me what happened . . .'

She lit her cigarette and took one or two puffs, calmly. 'I pulled up, of course. I got up and went round to the back of the car to see what had happened. It was quite obvious. Both my off-wheels had gone over his head.'

'Had you a torch?' asked the sergeant.

'No. And I didn't back my car either to get its headlights on to the thing. But there was a bit of a glow from the rear lamp and the night's quite clear. Stars, you know —very beautiful.'

'I suppose there was no one about who might have witnessed it?'

'Not one damned soul.'

The sergeant frowned. But Mrs Milne's gaze was back on the calendar. It told her that this was the fifth of January, or rather, since midnight had already passed, that yesterday had been the fifth of January.

'That car,' said the sergeant, 'that didn't dip its lights. What about that?'

She answered, turning tired eyes towards him again: 'It was out of sight before I'd even pulled up. It was some sort of a low sports car—I didn't notice it much.'

'And nobody else?'

'No one but me and my victim, sergeant. I took him by the heels and pulled him in to the side of the road. After all, I thought, there's no need for anyone else to run over him.'

'And you didn't recognize him as anyone local?'

'I did not. But I admit I left a more careful examination of his face to more competent people. It's a rough road and he was lying face downwards—there wasn't much face left.' Throwing her half-smoked cigarette at the stove, she added: 'He'd a brown tweed suit and his shoes needed soling.'

The sergeant rose. 'Then if that's all, us'll be gettin' along. You'd better come, ma'am, but you won't have to look at'n again if us can help it.'

Mrs Milne uncrossed her legs and planted her two feet firmly on the floor. 'I won't drive my car out there again,' she said, 'for any policeman with the whole dignity of the law behind him.'

'That's all right, ma'am,' said Eggbear patiently, 'Constable Leat will drive. Come on, Cecil.'

The night, as Mrs Milne had said, was clear and starry. It was frosty, too. Chovey's main street was empty, the street lamps shining on sleeping windows lidded with blinds. Chovey's shops were small; they left no lighted display for the unlikely latecomer. At the end of the street where hedges replaced cottages the road was deserted, a faint silvering of frost glinting on its surface in the beam of the headlights.

The car travelled on.

It passed the entrance to Mrs Milne's house, lying on the right. Farther on, Chovey Place, the big house of the neighbourhood, showed at intervals between gaps in the high hedge, its dark mass pricked with a few spots of light. A rabbit scuttled across the road ahead of the car.

The ambulance and the doctor had arrived before the police. Leat stopped the car at the nearer of the two bridges and he and the sergeant got out. The sergeant turned to tell Mrs Milne that perhaps she would not be needed, then he started down the road. Mrs Milne leant back in the car, shut her eyes, but immediately opened them again and, with nervous carelessness, lit herself another cigarette. The sergeant, glancing back over his shoulder, caught sight of the flare of the lighter inside the car, and the blur of a pale face above it.

'Twenty-seven and six,' he observed, 'and lived on it for a fortnight. Guess how much that fur coat her's wearing must have cost her.'

'Strikes me,' said the constable, 'us 'ere in Chovey don't know such a great amount about that lady.'

They crossed the bridge and turned, with the road, to the right, losing sight of the car.

This bridge was set at the first turn and the other bridge at the second of a sharp S-bend. Probably it was because the spot was so obviously dangerous that no accident had happened here before. Both bridges, built over streams that came together in the meadows to the right, were so narrow that only one car at a time could cross over, and so steeply humped that up to the moment when a car reached the middle, it was driving blind. Both bridges had low brick walls on either side of them. Between them the road was raised above the meadows with fences along each side. The ambulance was drawn up about half-way between the bridges, its lights turned on a figure that lay in the shallow ditch.

The doctor and two other men were standing beside it.

'Well, doctor, is he dead?' said Eggbear as he came up.

The doctor, a short man with heavy shoulders and a sallow, loose-skinned face, turned and nodded. He took his hands out of his pockets, blew on them, rubbed them together, stuck them into his pockets again and called it confounded weather.

'Tight?' said Eggbear.

' 'Spect so.'

'Then that lets the lady out.'

'Which lady?'

'Mrs Milne of The Laurels. 'Twas her car done him in.'

'Was it, indeed!' Dr Sanders uttered a sound from within his upturned coat-collar that might have been a chuckle.

'Somethin' funny?' said the sergeant. He had approached the body and was stooping over it.

'No,' said the doctor, 'of course not.'

'Never seen'n myself that I know of,' said Eggbear. ' 'Tis nobody local. D'you know'n, Cecil?'

'Not by them clothes,' said Leat.

'And there ain't much else to go on, eh?'

There was not. The man had evidently been lying face downwards on the road when the wheels of the car went over him. His face had been scraped and pulped against the gritty surface.

'Oldish man,' said Eggbear, 'his hair's turnin' grey.'

'There's a good whiff of whisky about him still,' said Dr Sanders. 'He can't have had it long ago. If you start inquiries in the pubs around you ought to be able to get a line on him.'

'I'd thought of that all on my lonesome,' answered Eggbear.

He put a hand into one pocket of the dead man's jacket and pulled out a half-empty packet of Woodbines, a match-box with only two matches left, a sixpenny piece and a halfpenny. He looked them over and returned them to the pocket. 'No one very *à la*,' he observed, straightening.

'The clothes tell you that.'

Eggbear nodded. The man's suit was of cheap brown tweed and fitted his long and bony figure awkwardly, his shirt was soiled and frayed, and his shoes, as Mrs Milne had said, were in bad need of soling.

'We'd better get'n back to the station,' Eggbear said, 'then go through his belongings proper, and see what they've got to tell us.'

'Right,' said the doctor, and turning to the two men who were with him, said: 'You can get him on board.'

'And Cecil, after you've driven us back you can drive Mrs Milne home again. She'd better not handle a car, the state she's in tonight.' He stepped aside so that the two men with the stretcher could get at the body.

The doctor thrust out a cigarette-case. 'Was Mrs Anna Milne of The Laurels in a state?'

'A bit of a state like—not near so bad as some'd be.'

'I suppose she wasn't drunk herself, by any chance?'

'No, sir,' said Leat positively, 'she was not. I can bear witness.'

'Doctor,' said the sergeant, 'I'll lay you half a crown it don't work the first time.'

'What, this lighter? I'll take you on. It's unusual, I know, but this happens to be an entirely satisfac— Tt, tt!' The doctor sighed and handed over two shillings. 'I'll owe you the sixpence. Come on, men, get going.'

CHAPTER 3

At about nine o'clock the next morning Cecil Leat dismounted from his bicycle outside the white-painted gate of The Laurels and wheeled his bicycle up the drive.

The morning was sharp and pleasant. On either side of him the dark leaves of the laurels gleamed with hoar-frost; the sky was a faint blue. The house ahead of him was of quiet grey stone, with long sash windows, its roof of slate, high-pitched. Ivy covered one side of it. Built too late in the last century to have much beauty, its solidity and lack of ostentation gave it dignity. Cecil Leat—he was twenty-three years old, big, sandy-haired and plump in the face—propped his bicycle against the porch, mounted two smartly whitened steps, and gave a sharp ring at the bell.

His cousin, Ruby Leat, opened it.

'Why, Cecil!' she said.

He stamped a little on the mat, rubbed his cold hands together, and asked if Mrs Milne were in.

'Aye,' said Ruby. She was tall, fair and round-faced like her cousin. 'She's in; I've just taken her breakfast up to her.'

'I've a question or two to ask,' said the constable, 'about the accident last night. So if you'll just ask her, Rube, if 'twill be convenient for she to see me . . .'

' 'Twon't be,' said Ruby. 'What accident?'

'Accident up over,' said Leat.

'But her's still in bed,' said Ruby. 'I told you, I just took her breakfast up to her. And you can't see Miss Daphne either; she's up to London.'

'Then please inquire when Mrs Milne will be good enough to see me.'

Ruby went upstairs. Soon she was down again and telling her cousin to come inside and wait. 'Mrs Milne will be down as soon as she can manage.' She took him into the drawing-room.

Cecil Leat walked to one of the windows and stood with his hands behind him, his back to the room. The windows reached from floor to ceiling, framed in curtains of a soft, fresh green; the carpet under his feet was grey, the walls were a colour between the green and the grey and quite without pictures; only above the fireplace there hung a gold-framed convex mirror. Looking over his shoulder to see why Ruby should have so much to do with the fire-irons, Leat caught sight of himself in this; it gave him a shock, it turned him to so strangely diminished a figure.

Ruby put more coal on the fire and went on fussing with the tongs and the poker until she had the whole story of the accident out of her cousin.

'D'you know what cook'll say?' she said. ' "I told 'e so' —that's what her'll say. Her's leavin' this day fortnight.'

'What, cook is?'

'Yes, given in her notice a couple of weeks back. And her'll say: "I told 'e so"—you take it from me. 'Er says that Mrs Milne is that reckless in all her habits that somethin's bound to happen—and now it has!'

'But 'twasn't Mrs Milne's fault, seemingly.'

'Well, cook'll say as 'twas. She says that Sir Joseph Maxwell was quite right to report Mrs Milne for dangerous driving.'

'Well, he wasn't, then,' said Leat. 'Us kept an eye on her, and her broke none of the regulations no more than most people. What's chasing cook away?'

'Because she says Mrs Milne is a—'

But at that moment Ruby sprang quickly to her feet and left the room. As she did so Mrs Milne came in.

She looked fresh enough this morning. In her brisk movements and pleasant smile she revealed no signs of strain. For all the marks her adventure had left upon her she might have been in bed by ten o'clock the previous evening and slept soundly all night. She wore a dark-red tailored suit; her dark hair was brushed smoothly back from her face and rolled up low on her neck. It all looked quiet, severe even, except for the flash of the rings on her fingers. Diamonds—a whole splash of them. Leat found himself staring at them before he looked at her face.

'I'm sorry to have kept you waiting,' she said. 'Do please sit down. Policemen standing about always make one's furniture look out of proportion.' She sat down herself and offered him a cigarette from an enamelled box. 'It's more questions, I suppose. We're some way, aren't we, from the end of the unpleasant business? There'll be an inquest?'

'Yes, ma'am. But at present 'tis this question of identification. You told us last night you didn't know the corpse.'

'Never been introduced to it in my life, that I can remember.'

'Well, ma'am,' said the constable, 'it seems as he knew you. He'd got your name and address on a piece of paper in his pocket.'

'Mine?'

'Yes, ma'am. "Mrs Anna Milne, The Laurels, Chovey." We found it in his inside pocket when we made a search of his clothing.' He extracted a piece of paper from between the leaves of his note-book and held it out. 'You weren't expectin' anyone to visit you maybe—anyone you didn't know by sight?'

She shook her head as she took the paper. She looked at it on both sides.

'This is a shop receipt,' she said, 'the sort of thing you stick in your pocket and forget about.'

'Yes, ma'am.'

'A shop somewhere in Cape Town'. She turned it over again and looked at her own name and address written on the back in pencilled capitals. 'I come from South Africa,' she said. 'You probably know that.'

'So the sergeant heard tell.'

She looked at him, and Constable Leat, who found her eyes disturbing, looked back at her flashing rings. Mrs Milne fluttered the paper between her fingers.

'But this man—this man I killed. I suppose there's no doubt that I did kill him? He wasn't dead already, by any chance?'

'We'll get the doctor's report later in the day, ma'am.'

She seemed to feel his gaze upon her jewels, for she started twisting them round. She said with increased harshness: 'So he's South African.'

'Well, ma'am, all his clothes come from there, and what with this receipt and your name on it . . .'

'Yes, yes, my name. But it's a very long time since I left South Africa—fifteen years or so.'

'You've no friends who might maybe have sent him along to you?'

'I don't think so. I've lost touch with them all. There isn't one I still correspond with. Of course, I can't be sure. But really—' her voice was staccato—'I can't think of anyone there to whom I've given my present address.'

'And you're quite, quite sure, ma'am, that the man himself was unknown to you?'

'As sure as the darkness and my own nerves would let me be.'

'Then if you wouldn't mind . . .'

'No, I don't mind taking a good look at him by daylight. Straight after breakfast, though! Still, I'll do as you wish. But I can't think of anyone—*anyone*—who fits the part. He was a biggish man, wasn't he? I realized that when I pulled him to the side. And thinnish. And middle-aged.'

'Yes, and pretty down and out by the look of him. His clothes wouldn't have done him much longer, supposin' he'd lived, and he'd only sixpence-ha'penny on him. Sergeant wondered whether maybe 'twas a man been sent to you to ask for work or a helpin' hand like.'

'Perhaps,' she said, 'perhaps.' And she stood up, repeating in a tone that had a flatly deliberate sound: 'But I can't think of anyone who could have sent him.'

That was what she stuck to when, soon after, she found herself looking at the body. No, she had never seen the man before, and though it was not impossible that some old acquaintance had given the man her name and address so that she might help him, she could think of no one who was in fact likely to have done so.

Going very white when she saw the body, she said: 'You realize, Sergeant, I'm not exactly practised at recognizing people in this sort of condition.' Then, after a long and almost fascinated look at the mutilated face: 'No, I'm sorry, but I can't help you.'

Afterwards, as Sergeant Eggbear was accompanying her to the street, she asked a number of questions about how the police were setting about the identifying of the dead man. He told her: 'Well, we'm makin' the usual inquiries round about, and a description of him is bein' broadcast. Also we'm askin' the driver of the other car, the low sports car you mentioned, to come forward. It shouldn't be difficult to pick up some kind of lead. You see, he was drunk, so he must have been seen in a pub not far away like as not.'

She nodded, looking down at the ground. Suddenly she shivered as if the frost had just penetrated the defences of her fur coat.

'And while I think of it,' said the sergeant, 'there's somethin' else I been wonderin' about, and maybe you could tell me. You dropped Major Maxwell at the crossroads, didn't you?'

'Yes,' she replied.

'Then maybe Major Maxwell saw the man come by.'

'What if he did?'

'Only that he'd have seen the face in its normal condition, and could give us a description. We reckon the man must've come down the road from Purbrook; no one in the pubs here saw'n, no more did the man on the railway crossing on the Plymouth road, no more did the AA man at the crossroads lower down. He must've come from Purbrook. So if the major chanced to look up and down when you dropped him, maybe he saw him.'

'I see,' she said. 'But I shouldn't think he did. I saw Major Maxwell climb over the stile and go off towards his cottage. It was a cold night, you know, not the sort of night for loitering about, particularly after a hot evening's badminton.'

'No, ma'am. Still, there'd be no harm in askin'.'

'Oh, no,' she said, 'no harm.'

She gave him a smile and went a few steps across the pavement towards her car. But she paused once more.

'When's the inquest?' she asked.

'Thursday afternoon.'

'Thursday.' She climbed into the car. 'And if you haven't got your identification by then?'

'We may have to ask for an adjournment.'

Again the constable and his bicycle approached the house of Mrs Milne. But this time, instead of stopping there, they continued straight on.

It was two o'clock and by now the wintry sunshine had infused some warmth into the day; the morning's white crust of frost had disappeared, and in the hedges the twigs were shining with a coating of damp.

The face of Cecil Leat reddened and his pedalling lost some of its fierceness; he answered good day to the people who passed him, and, meeting the vicar, he dismounted and had a chat with him. A cawing of rooks, a dripping of water from the tips of branches, the occasional noise of a shotgun or a passing car made up the texture of the afternoon's sounds. Five or six miles off the hills of Dartmoor, edging the sky with their smooth curves, had a look of gaiety, the pattern of meadow and ploughland, copse and winding road, showing up with a pale, bright clarity.

Presently Cecil Leat and his bicycle turned off to the left. A winding road brought him, after about ten minutes, to some gates, tall gates of wrought iron. Beyond them stretched an avenue of beeches. Leat edged his bicycle through the gates, remounted and resumed his placid pedalling. This was the drive of Chovey Place where Sir Joseph and Lady Maxwell lived with what was considered in Chovey a rather penurious number of servants. Major Maxwell, Sir Joseph's brother, lived in a cottage on the estate.

A lane, branching out of the avenue and dipping past a farm, then twisting and climbing again, brought Leat to the cottage. He arrived just as the major was starting out across the fields towards the manor. A dog noticed the arrival of the constable first and proclaimed it with the noisiness of one who takes an indiscriminate pleasure in strangers. It was a young and whimsical-eyed Aberdeen. The major turned, saw the constable, and came and leant on his garden gate.

'Afternoon, Leat. What can I do for you?'

Stuart Maxwell was a man of about fifty. He was tall. His hair, that had once been black, was now of that greyness that has an almost bluish-silver sheen. The arched eyebrows were still black; like the straight features and the fine wrinkles in his skin, they were clearly defined. It was one of those faces that look as if they have been drawn by a hard pencil.

Leaning on the gate, he took out his pipe and began to fill it. He was wearing gum-boots, over the tops of which bulged flannel trousers. Both the flannels and the loose jacket, made of what had been one of the more cheerful sorts of check, had their pattern of muddy paw-marks.

'I suppose you've heard about the accident last night, sir?' said Cecil Leat.

The major shook his head.

'Accident between two bridges up over,' said Leat.

'No,' said the major. 'Somebody killed?'

'Yes, sir—run over by Mrs Milne.'

'Good heavens.' But the words were without any noticeable emotion. 'When?' He cupped his hands round his pipe and lit it.

'Shortly after dropping you at the crossroads, sir. The man's unknown.'

'And what do you want me to do about it?'

Cecil Leat took a faintly wondering look at Major Maxwell before he replied. For there was gossip in Chovey about Major Maxwell and Mrs Milne; yet the major could hardly have taken less interest in her accident, even if, as was incredible, the gossip had had nothing in it.

'I called to inquire,' said Leat, 'if maybe you didn't happen to see someone comin' along the road just after you'd been put down—see them well enough to give us a bit of a description. 'Tis the difficulty of identifying the body, sir.'

One of Stuart Maxwell's hands went down to scratch the ear of his Aberdeen. 'No,' he said, 'I don't think I did.'

'No one on the road from Purbrook?'

'No-o.' His voice was deep and rather indistinct; it had a drawling, lazy sound. 'As a matter of fact, if there had been anyone I should certainly have seen him. I remember I glanced up that way—I remember it distinctly now—and saw a car's headlights a good way off. If anyone had been coming down the road I should have seen him against them.'

'What kind of car?' asked Leat.

'Oh, I didn't see. It branched off towards Plymouth. No, I'm sorry I can't say anything to help you.'

'I suppose, sir, at the time of the accident itself you were already at home? I suppose you didn't hear anything?'

A quick grin appeared for a moment on Stuart Maxwell's face, but there was a rasp in his drawl as he said: 'Really, Leat, d'you imagine I'd have left Mrs Milne to handle a gruesome business like that by herself if I'd had the faintest idea of what was happening? No, Mrs Milne dropped me at the crossroads, went down the other way to drop Miss Willis, and can't have passed the spot again for at least ten minutes—time for me to have got home, got the house locked up and got myself a drink. It's barely five minutes' walk across the fields to the Purbrook road from here, you know.'

'That's just it, sir. 'Tis odd, to my way of thinkin', that the lady never called you, seein' you live so close by.'

The grin appeared again, staying longer this time. The major remarked quietly: 'D'you know, that sounds as if you don't believe me. What's on your mind, Leat? What's worrying you? Have you any reason for thinking I might be expected not to tell the truth?'

A stolid shake of the head was the constable's reply. 'All the same—'

'It's not in the least odd,' Stuart Maxwell went on, 'if you're at all well acquainted with Mrs Milne.'

'No, sir. All the same . . .' But in the end Leat did not produce his comment. He thanked the major for having answered his questions, flung a leg over his saddle and pedalled away.

The major stood staring after him for a long moment.

When Cecil Leat reached the police station the sergeant greeted him: 'Well, Cecil, my lad, here's another trip for you and your bike. Get along out to the scene of yesterday's accident—'

'God, Sergeant, that's just where I been!'

'That's right, Cecil, you—'

'Not five minutes' walk away!'

'Ah, but you couldn't've done then what you belong to do now. I didn't know meself till now what 'twas you belonged to be doin'. For I've just this moment had an idea. Get along out where we was last night, and have a good look round for a bottle.'

'What of?'

'A bottle, or a flask it might be, which your nose tells you used to contain whisky. 'Tis this way. Us been telephonin' all the pubs here and in to Purbrook, and in to Wallaford too, but us can't get no line on the bloke. Then along comes doctor and tells us this: the bloke's stomach is fair swimmin' in whisky. Straight whisky—it ain't been absorbed at all. And that means, says doctor, 'e must've gulped it down only a moment afore 'e was killed. And that means, says I, 'e must've had somethin' to gulp it down out of. So you're booked for that bottle, my lad. You get along out and find it.'

Cecil Leat looked sourly at the self-congratulation on the sergeant's face. 'Scotland Yard!' He laughed cheerlessly.

CHAPTER 4

Although the road on which the accident had happened was the shortest route from Chovey to Purbrook, there was seldom much traffic upon it. Winding and narrow, it turned driving into a constant caution, a tiresome concentration. Another road, the main road to Wallaford, that unrolled like a piece of stair-carpet over the undulations of the countryside, was, in spite of its indirectness, the more popular. So the sight of a police constable squelching about in the swampy meadows at the side of the road and picking up pieces of broken glass and smelling them, collected no audience, during the first half-hour or so, except one man with a bicycle, one woman with a perambulator, two boys, and a baker's van. Soon even those dispersed.

Leat had first searched the sides of the road itself. But the hedges and ditches had yielded only a few rusty tins and decayed ice-cream cartons. Climbing down then at the end of one of the bridges, he had continued his search in the sucking, oozing grass of the meadows and along the sides of the streams. Using a piece of stick to stir up the mud and pebbles, he searched the streams themselves. It was a lugubrious but thorough examination.

The constable's waterproof cape, spread on the grass, received all his finds. It was at the moment when, having picked up almost under one of the bridges a beer bottle of more obvious newness than any of the others, he was starting to carry this towards his dump, that he heard a voice above his head inquire: 'What d'you think he's doing, George?'

'Layin' the cloth for a picnic.'

Cecil Leat looked up and saw two faces looking down at him over the edge of the brick parapet.

He saw two pairs of elbows. Above the elbows two pairs of hands supported, in the one case a long, narrow chin with a cleft in it, in the other a broad, chubby chin with a dimple. The long chin went with a hooked nose, a swarthy skin and a lock of dark hair falling almost into one of a pair of slightly slanting, dark eyes. The chubby chin formed part of a pink and plastic-looking mass, approximately circular, that looked as if features had been shaped in it by the gentle pressing here and there of tentative fingers. The dark face was ferocious, dramatic; its owner wore a shirt of a dull crimson, no tie, no hat and a new waterproof of pale parchment colour. The pink face nestled between a greasy blue cap and the high neck of a sailor's jersey.

Curious, they watched Leat. It was the pink faced man who first joined in the search. Pushing his way between the hedge and the parapet, he slithered down the bank into the meadow and began looking for glass. Presently the other followed. Silently, looking round at Leat from time to time for reference, they copied his actions, bringing any fragments they found to add to the pile on the waterproof cape. They tried smelling the pieces as well, and this, after a while made the dark man say to the policeman in passing: 'If you'd tell us what trail it is you're trying to pick up it'd be a good deal easier.'

Leat looked at him. 'Seen you before somewhere haven't I?'

'Not impossible,' said the dark man.

'I know as 'tisn't,' said Leat. 'I know I seen you.'

The fair man gave a quick tug at the other's sleeve. 'Here,' he began anxiously. But the dark man grinned. Standing face to face with him, it could be seen that he was as tall as the constsable. His age might have been thirty-three.

'I can't recall where,' said Cecil Leat, 'but I know I seen you.'

'Here—'

'Shut up, George. Overcome your fear of the law.' He grinned again. 'Won't you tell us what smell it is that you're trying to smell?'

Leat admitted it: 'Whisky.'

George gave a little giggle. Shrugging away from the restraining hand, he wandered off to look for more pieces of broken bottle. Leat went on: 'A bloke was done in on the road here last night—run over. Don't know who he was and got to find out. Doctor says as his stomach was a-swim in whisky, so—'

'Oh, I see,' said the other rapidly. 'Logical, conscientious —there must be a bottle. And a bottle can't lie—if it tells you anything, which isn't at all certain. Still, even if it doesn't, there must be a bottle.'

Leat nodded slowly. 'Only,' he said, 'there ain't.'

One eyebrow on the dark face raised itself suddenly as if it had been hooked up by a question-mark. Leat shrugged his shoulders and turned once more to his search.

But no bottle was found. No bottle, that is to say, that was new enough and fragrant enough. Not a sniff of whisky did Cecil Leat or either of the strangers enjoy until nearly ten o'clock that evening, and that was not on the Purbrook road, but in the bar of the Ring of Bells in Chovey. Even then Cecil Leat was out of it.

It was Major Maxwell who ordered the whisky. Only beer had been drunk by the couple of farmers, the sexton, the auctioneer, the postman and the others who had gathered in the bar. But when Major Maxwell came in, accompanied by Mrs Milne and a young man called Adrian Laws, who was some sort of cousin of the Maxwells, it was Scotch that the major demanded for the three of them. Tensely, explosively, with a thump of his lean fist on the bar, he demanded Scotch.

Adrian Laws leant over the bar and murmured to George Warren, who stood behind it, that they had been dining at the Place. 'Cauliflower au gratin, figs, custard, and a double orange juice apiece,' he added. He was a tall young man with slightly stooping shoulders; his smooth, oval face and spectacles gave him a faint resemblance to a Chinese student at the London School of Economics, only his hair was reddish, a curling, shining, untidily worn crown of copper. Behind the horn-rimmed glasses the eyes were greenish.

'Ah, reckon you can do with a drink after an evenin' up to the Place,' said Tom Warren with a wink. His bar was a low-ceilinged room, papered in a warm and frowsy red, with a fire of logs ablaze on the wide hearth, and with warmly, stickily gleaming varnish on the furniture. On the floor red linoleum, patterned in an imitation of tiles, hid the tiles that were actually below it. King Edward and Queen Alexandra gazed fadedly from above the fireplace. 'Reckon it makes you feel cold in your innards, the Place these days,' said Tom, and looking round him, added: 'I'm all for good food and drink and cheerful surroundings.'

Softly Major Maxwell remarked to Mrs Milne: 'Adrian's told the village so much about the austerities and earnest moralities of my good brother that I believe they're as much discussed and quite as scandalously enjoyed as the debts and lecheries of the family he bought the place from. I'll bet there's not a man in this room who doesn't know that my sister-in-law chews raw oatmeal for breakfast.'

She nodded, giving a smile that made little pretence of amusement; in some way, indeed, it only made her face more tired. She had hitched herself on to one of the high stools by the bar, leaning an elbow on the counter's shiny top. The long skirt of her dull blue satin dress draped its folds about the stool with what, in that place, was a faintly comic graciousness; her fur coat hung open, showing flowers on her breast.

'Oh, yes,' she said, drawing her glass towards her with a gesture heavy in its listlessness, 'Adrian loves a good gossip. He has a nicer name for it, I expect—picking up local colour or something.' Her voice had an edge to it, as of acute but weary irritation.

Stuart Maxwell regarded her for a moment, his eyes speculative. She turned away from him and looked at the room. In profile the hardness of her face was very apparent. Lifting the drink he had demanded with such demonstrative impatience, the major sipped it absent-mindedly, his eyes turning cloudily to King Edward and Queen Alexandra.

'You know,' Adrian Laws murmured to him, in the soft, confidential voice that was often to be heard in the Ring of Bells, 'I'm not responsible for the story about the hair-shirt.'

'Hair-shirt?' said the major.

'It's got around that the only underclothing Joe wears is a hair-shirt. I was just explaining, I'm not responsible for it.'

'Who is?' said the major.

Adrian gave a meaning look at Mrs Milne's profile, then looked back at the major, his lips twitching.

'Anna?' said the major. 'Don't believe it.'

'Of course not,' said Adrian, 'but what about the young of the species—Daphne. The story has a certain immaturity, don't you think?'

The major gave an obliging but abstracted smile. Just then he felt a sharp tug at his sleeve.

'Stuart, look!' said Mrs Milne. Her fingers, when they took hold of anything, seemed naturally to take a decisive hold; his sleeve, as she tugged at it, looked as if it must be her property as much as his. 'That man,' she said, 'and the other. Watch them, it's rather beautiful.'

Some men round the skittles board had begun to get drunk and were being amusing. One, who wore a crimson shirt, a swarthy fellow with sleek, dark hair and a flashing smile, was actually tap-dancing. Two farmers, the sexton, a purple-faced auctioneer and the pouchy-eyed, plus-four-clad veterinary surgeon were watching with grinning interest and admiration.

Anna Milne's tight lips relaxed as she watched. From behind the bar Tom Warren leant forward and whispered:

'The little feller in blue kept beatin' him at skittles, although he'd all sorts of fancy tricks with the ball, and kept complainin' about its weight and all that. I reckon he's started dancin' to show there's somethin' he can do better.'

The group round the skittles board was cheering the dancer. Suddenly he stopped, said: 'Show you how to tap-dance,' and repeated the performance.

Anna Milne looked round at Adrian.

'Lots of atmosphere for you tonight,' she remarked.

Something sardonic appeared on his bland, oval face. 'Which is the worse, Anna, a self-conscious hunt for atmosphere, or a pretence that the atmosphere's natural to you, a pretence that you belong to it?'

She jerked her head away, as if his breath had tickled her.

Out in the middle of the red linoleum the feet of the dancer were drumming a rhythm like the keys of a typewriter. He flung his arms around him in florid gestures. One of the farmers began to sing a song that had been dance-music when he was young; it pinned itself saggingly to the brisk clatter of the dancing feet. The purple-faced auctioneer clapped his hand on the shoulder of the little man in blue. 'Can you do that?' he asked.

The little man came forward dubiously.

The little man's feet began to move delicately. His companion in the red shirt stepped back and leant against the bar. The little man made a few inconspicuous movements, a sudden loud clatter with his heels, flung up a hand and struck the side of his head, stood erect and smiled chubbily. There was a burst of applause.

'Wit, that's what does it,' said Adrian Laws enthusiastically.

Red-shirt turned away and groaned.

It was some time before the little man was allowed to stop his dancing. Repetition after repetition was demanded from him, not variations, not originality, but simply that one flash of humour over and over again. At last the auctioneer gave him another clap on the shoulder.

'Where did you learn that?' he inquired.

'Old sailor-man,' was the mumbled answer.

'Where d'you come from?' the auctioneer continued.

'Yes, where d'you come from?' asked one of the farmers. 'You bain't English, be 'e?'

'Never see an Englishman do that,' said the auctioneer.

'No, never see an Englishman do that,' said the farmer.

The little man looked from one to the other. He seemed slow at understanding. The sexton prompted him: 'You bain't a Turk, be 'e?'

There was a howl of laughter. The auctioneer said: 'You're American, aren't you? Or Danish—that's what you look like. Or Norwegian. Something like that.'

Red-shirt observed drearily: 'You've got him all wrong. He's a Jap.'

In the midst of more laughter the little man answered slowly: 'Ever heard of a little place called Princetown, about a dozen miles from a little place called Chovey? There's a prison there. That's where I come from.'

Nobody believed him, not even Sergeant Eggbear who came in at that moment.

The first thing the sergeant did on entering the bar that Wednesday evening was to walk to the wireless and switch it on. His action let into the room a rich, deep voice that announced gravely:

' "Here lies a wretched corse, of wretched soul bereft:
Seek not my name: a plague consume you wicked
caitiffs left! . . ." '

Then, with good evenings left and right, the sergeant advanced to the bar and ordered a pint of bitter. Just as the wireless was telling the room to ' "Pass by, and curse thy fill . . ." ' he looked round and noticed who it was that was standing beside him.

It was the dark-haired man in the red shirt.

'Toby Dyke!'

' "Dead is noble Timon," ' said the wireless.

The man in the red shirt said: 'Hullo, Sammy, nice to see you again,' and looked as if he were going to burst into tears.

'Toby Dyke,' said the sergeant, reaching out both hands to grasp one of the other man's limp ones and shake it vigorously. 'I've always said, one day sooner or later, Toby Dyke'll turn up here again. Haven't I, Tom?'

Tom Warren nodded and the wireless said: ' "Let our drums strike," ' and then was silent.

In the bar there was a shifting of places, an ordering of drinks. Major Maxwell took a cigarette-case out of his pocket and offered it to his two companions. But Mrs Milne was taking a mirror out of her bag, staring into it and frowning, and Adrian Laws was taking a long look at the man called Toby Dyke and at Sergeant Eggbear.

These two were being looked at by most of the people in the room. Only the small man in the blue jersey had drifted away from the crowd to pick up a handful of darts and start throwing them with an undemonstrative style but with spectacular accuracy at the board in the corner.

'This,' the wireless resumed, 'is the late news—Exchange Telegraph, Reuter, Central News, copyright reserved. First there is a police message. Will anyone able to give information leading to the identification of a middle-aged man who was run over by a car and fatally injured on the road between Chovey and Purbrook—?'

Mrs Milne's hands lay still in her lap. A moment ago her fingers had been twisting round the handle of her small mesh bag, but now they lay quite still. Suddenly she got to her feet.

'That's enough of that,' she said, and twitching her fur coat closely round her, walked quickly to the door.

Stuart Maxwell followed her immediately. In the doorway he paused for a moment to turn and meet the eyes of Sergeant Eggbear, who appeared, like several others, to have been startled by this abrupt withdrawal. The wireless was continuing with a description of the clothes of the man who had been run over the night before, and asking anyone who might have information to give to communicate with the chief constable of the county. The major looked at the sergeant with an expression on his face that no one there had ever seen before. Anger can make a face, even one that has been disciplined by the British army, burn with an astonishing, a blazing, cruel vitality.

The major went out. Adrian Laws swivelled round on his high, varnished stool and murmured: 'Now you wouldn't call that tactful, would you, sergeant?'

The sergeant started drumming with his large hand on the bar.

'Not a nice look, was it?' said Toby Dyke. 'What've you done, Sam?'

The sergeant muttered and swore.

Adrian Laws said: 'Rubbed a very sore place.' He had edged himself into the group with the sergeant and the stranger. 'Last night, you see, our Mrs Milne knocked a man down with her car and killed him. Tonight the sergeant goes and switches on the wireless so that she can hear her error being made public to the world. She didn't like it.'

'Did you do it on purpose, Sam?' said Toby Dyke.

'What, me?' said the sergeant. 'I didn't even see her!'

'Just wanted to listen in to the sort of mess a BBC announcer would make of pronouncing a couple of names like Chovey and Purbrook?' Toby Dyke patted him on the shoulder. 'Does make you feel right at the centre of things, doesn't it?' Across the sergeant's darkened face he winked at Adrian Laws.

'I say, Sergeant,' said Adrian, 'won't you introduce me to your friend? I've heard such a lot about him from you; I've always hoped I'd come across him some time.'

'And that reminds me,' said Toby Dyke, 'I've got a friend to introduce. George!'

But as George turned round, a bunch of darts in his fist and a look of shyness on his face, a constable appeared in the doorway and started chirruping from there to the sergeant. Eggbear walked across to him.

' 'Tis a call come in for you,' said the constable, 'about the accident. There's a woman in to Wallaford says she heard the message on the wireless and she phoned up to once. They've put her through to us. She says a man answering to the description given stayed at her house last night. She runs a boarding-house in Francis Street.'

'And can she tell us who he was?'

'We-ell,'' the constable hesitated. 'She's got his name. Or so she says. And maybe 'tis nought but a coincidence like. But still, strikes me as—'

'Get on with it,' said the sergeant, 'get on with it!'

The constable took a look past him at the people in the room. Some were going on with their talk, their drinks or their skittles, but a few, Toby Dyke for one, and Adrian Laws and George were frankly listening. Besides, in all that talk, that drinking and playing, there was something, some unnaturalness. The intentness of curiosity was on nearly every face.

The constable tweaked the sergeant's sleeve and drew him outside.

CHAPTER 5

In the police station the sergeant sat looking at the notes he had taken of his conversation over the telephone with the police sergeant in Wallaford.

'Well,' he said, 'I reckon Maxwell ain't such an out of the common name as all that. Maybe, as you say, 'tis just a coincidence like.'

He tapped his teeth with his pencil.

From over his shoulder the long arm of Toby Dyke reached down and tweaked away the sheet of notes. It had happened that at the moment when the constable drew Sergeant Eggbear out of the bar Tom Warren turned down the lights and started talking about time. So Toby had followed the sergeant. Reluctantly, and keeping a yard or two behind, George had followed Toby. George now sat on a chair by the stove, his cap on his knees, his manner embarrassed, as if he felt that everyone was looking at him.

The sergeant's notes were unintelligible. Toby gave them back to him.

'What's it all about, Sam?'

Before answering the question the sergeant asked: 'You still a newspaper reporter, Toby, like you were when we first met?'

'Why?'

'Are you or ain't you?'

'I'm not. Living by my wits—and George's. Why?'

The sergeant gazed ahead of him with a heavy stare. 'Bein' the way it is,' he said slowly, 'I reckon us don't want this in the papers—yet.' He turned his stare up at the narrow, hook-nosed face. 'There's some men,' he said, 'you can't trust not to put their jobs before everythin' else.'

Toby Dyke grinned. 'Well, get on with it. I've told you it isn't my job any more.'

'Then 'tis this way,' said the sergeant. 'Last night Mrs Milne, the lady you see in to the Ring o' Bells, she runs over a man and kills'n. Comes straight here and tells us about it. She don't know who 'tis, and none of us don't recognize'n. You heard on the wireless what kind o' man he was. He was drunk and his clothes weren't none too good and he'd just sixpence-ha'penny on him. His face was nought to go upon—'twasn't there, for the most part. But there was a bit o' paper in his pocket, stuck away in a corner like, a check for somethin' he'd bought. Cape Town was where that came from. Well, Mrs Milne's a South African lady—and there's her name and address written on the back o' this check. But she goes on sayin' as she never seen nor heard of'n. Well, then, I get that announcement on the wireless . . .'

'And your answer comes in right away.' Toby Dyke sat down on a corner of the table. 'Bit of luck,' he remarked, but he made it sound like a question.

'Aye,' said the sergeant, also doubtfully.

On his chair by the stove George made a little coughing sound, as if he wished to draw attention to something he intended to say.

But before he had begun it the sergeant was continuing: 'A woman in to Wallaford, a Mrs Quantick by name, as keeps a boardin'-house in Francis Street—that ain't one o' the best streets—her phones up to say that on Monday night a man answering to the description on the wireless occupied one o' the rooms in her house. He left in the mornin', carryin' a suitcase.'

The constable put in: 'Where's the suitcase to now, then?'

'How do I know?' snapped Eggbear. 'How do I know if 'tis the same man? We'll be fetchin' Mrs Quantick over tomorrow to see if her can identify him. Till then . . . But still,' he added, 'this is what she tells us. When he went off with his suitcase—'twas a leather suitcase, with initials stamped on it—when he went off he left a coat behind as he forgot to pack, seemingly. 'Tis hangin' in the cupboard on a hanger, and in the pocket, her says, there's some papers and a handkerchief and a passport. And the passport's the property of one Shelley Maxwell.' He broke off and looked up again at Toby Dyke. 'Plenty of people in the world called Maxwell.'

'But there can't be many people who'd put Shelley in front of it,' said Toby. 'Go on, Sam, who is it you don't want it to be. I'm not up in your local politics.'

'Did you see that man in the bar, Toby, that gave me that look?'

Toby nodded.

'Well, that's Major Stuart Maxwell, and he's the brother of Sir Joseph Maxwell, and Sir Joseph Maxwell's the owner of Chovey Place, and I'm just thinkin' . . .'

'I can guess the sort of thing you're thinking, Sam. But where does Shelley come in?'

The sergeant sighed. 'Maxwells ain't a local family,' he said, 'I don't know everything about'n. 'Tis round twenty year or so back that Sir Joseph bought the Place. In those days there was a son. He wasn't here much o' the time; he was in some kind of a job up to London—Sir Joseph'd never be one to let a son idle, no matter how much money there was. He'd be down for a weekend now and then, or sometimes longer. A wild one he was; he was a daddy for the girls and liked to go on the tiddly. More than once there was stories of the trouble he had with his father. And then, all to once, he stopped comin'. Vanished. Lots o' people asked questions. There was some stories too . . .' He hesitated. 'I always allowed as he'd had a big row with his old man over somethin' and got thrown out.'

'And was his name Shelly?'

The sergeant gave a troubled shake of his head. 'I can't remember as I ever heard his name. Folk always called'n by a kind of nickname—Bish, they called'n. Short for Bishop, I reckon, because a bishop was what he wasn't like.'

'No,' said Toby, 'I'm afraid not, Sam. That wasn't the reason. And I'm afraid his real name was Shelley.'

'Think so?' The sergeant sighed again. 'Not as it's anythin' to me, one way or the other, but 'tis the devil's own job when you've any o' these big people in on a case. Seem to think the law wasn't meant for them.' He swore wearily.

Toby Dyke thrust back the black lock that curved down into his eye. It immediately fell down again. 'Have you got that check about you, Sam, the one that was found in the man's pocket?'

'Why?' said the sergeant, but he produced it in the automatic way of a man who is worried and tired.

' "Mrs Milne, The Laurels, Chovey." Mrs Milne—that's the woman who was in the bar, you say, the one in the blue dress. Must have been good-looking not so very many years ago—still is, if it comes to that. But tough—got a bit tough with the passing of time, eh, Sam? And who was the man who was with her?'

'Major Maxwell.'

'No, the other one—the young one who stayed behind.'

Yawning, the sergeant answered: 'That was Mr Laws. Relative of the Maxwells.'

'What does he do?'

'Writes books.'

'What kind of books?'

'How should I know?'

Toby Dyke handed back the check. 'Well, so far as I can see, Sam—this is my serious opinion—there's going to be a certain amount of fun in the neighbourhood during the next few days. Or, as you might say, drama. Perhaps George and I will stay to see a little of it. We're just taking a holiday, walking about and looking at things. George needs a holiday; he's been indoors a lot too much lately—got no colour in his cheeks. What's that you say, George?' For George had made his little coughing noise again.

Wringing his cap between his hands in a bashful fashion, George gave it as his opinion that it was time to go to bed.

Having told Tom Warren that he and his friend would like their breakfast at half-past eight, Toby Dyke came down to eat it at half-past eleven.

Even then he had not shaved. With bristles on his chin and an unfed irritability in his eye, his long, dark face looked truculent and dangerous. He made impatient gestures, opening and shutting the door of the coffee-room noisily and scraping his chair on the floor as he pulled it out from under the table, as if it were not he but the breakfast that was late. George was sitting on the window-seat, reading a newspaper.

The coffee-room was a genteel room with white table-cloths on small round tables and some potted palms. Each table had a thin glass vase at its centre, filled with twigs on to which had been wired large, rubbery-looking berries, like small oranges. Most of the tables had already been laid for luncheon; only Toby's had an anachronistic toast-rack and teacup.

He was without friendliness towards the fried egg that was brought to him. He was sour towards the tea. Towards George he appeared without emotions of any kind. George stayed behind his newspaper.

It was about half an hour later that the first remark came. 'You know, George, you've got a nose.'

George flattened the palm of one hand against his face.

'Yes,' he said doubtfully, 'not a fine one like yours, Tobe.'

'You smell things out, don't you, George?' Toby had pushed his chair back, stretched his legs out, and was smoking. 'You realized the possibilities of that policeman picking primroses in the meadow. You went and helped him, and so found out what it was all about. Now I should merely have speculated and passed on.'

'Well, I reckon you'd have made as good use of your speculating as I shall of my knowing.'

Toby nodded. 'But the concrete mind comes in useful sometimes.'

'I've even known the solid brick kind come in useful—sometimes,' said George.

Toby did not answer. Blowing smoke at the oranges, he gazed at them as through a veil. 'We'll stay here a day or two,' he said presently.

George shrugged. 'Only . . .' he began with a faint frown.

'What?'

'I've been wondering. You told that sergeant of yours you hadn't got a job on that paper any more.'

'I haven't.'

'But they print all you send 'em.'

Toby rose, stretched himself and grinned. George turned the pages of his newspaper. Toby said he would go and shave. A girl in a darned jumper and shapeless skirt came in and asked if she could clear away the breakfast now. Past the windows of the coffee-room of the Ring of Bells a large car drove slowly and stopped a little farther down the street outside the police station. George noticed it out of the corner of his eye, but he went on reading.

When, about half an hour later, Toby and George emerged together into the street, the car was still there. But as they strolled towards the police station a man came out and got hastily into the car. Sergeant Eggbear had followed him out; there was respect in the sergeant's attitude, also gravity and concern. The car was driven away by a uniformed chauffeur at a rate of about fifteen miles an hour.

The man of whom Toby and George had caught this glimpse was tall, extremely thin and bearded. His face was yellowish. He looked an old man, but the beard was not yet grey, and he had crossed the pavement in one spidery stride.

'Well, that's that,' the sergeant greeted them.

'And that,' said Toby, with a nod after the car, 'was old man Maxwell?'

'That's right.' The sergeant retreated into the station and the other two followed him. 'We've cleared it up. It's his son—he says so. Not been seen or heard of for ten years, comes home and gets done in before he's seen any of his folks. Poor devil.'

'Has it cut the old man up?'

'You couldn't tell with him.' Eggbear pointed at a small pile of papers on his table. 'Those are his. Here's his passport. We had the landlady over from Wallaford this morning and she identified him as the man who stayed at her place.'

'What about the suitcase?' Toby had taken the passport and was looking at the photograph inside. It was faintly familiar, a flattish face with high cheekbones and a smooth, oval outline. But it was the kind of photograph that is obviously a bad photograph, a mere record of a set of features. 'Same type as his young cousin Laws,' Toby remarked.

'Yes, to look at.'

'Not otherwise?'

'No, Mr Laws is a quiet sort of chap. But folk still grin and start tellin' you yarns if you talk about Bish Maxwell. Well, 'tis an end o' the grinnin' now, I allow.'

'Er,' said George tentatively from somewhere behind Toby, 'the suitcase . . .'

'Ah,' said Eggbear, 'us haven't found'n yet.'

'Tried the railway cloakroom?' Toby inquired. He had put the passport down and was looking through the other papers. They were of the usual type that collect in a man's pocket, bills, receipts, a pamphlet of the kind that gets given away in the street and thrust into a pocket without being read.

There was a slight stiffness in the sergeant's answer: 'That did happen to have occurred to me meself. But as Mrs Quantick in to Wallaford had only just been and gone when Sir Joseph blows in, and as Sir Joseph had only just been and gone when you blows in . . .'

'Yes, yes,' said Toby.

'I'm goin' to do some phonin' about it now,' said the sergeant.

'There's the steamship company too,' said Toby. 'You might make sure that . . .' But he was stopped by the look of stern reproach on Eggbear's face.

While the sergeant, pulling the telephone squarely in front of him, entered into conversation with the police in Wallaford, Toby picked up the navy blue jacket that was hanging over the back of a chair and started looking idly through its pockets. He found nothing but a handkerchief and a stub of pencil, but he interrupted the sergeant to ask which pocket it was that had contained the bundle of papers. Eggbear told him that they had been folded up inside the passport in the inside pocket.

'No, Jim,' he went on into the telephone again, 'that was to a bloke this end. 'Tis a suitcase, accordin' to the description we have, a leather suitcase, good but pretty old, and probably deposited—'

But where that suitcase had probably been deposited was not at that moment imparted to the sergeant in Wallaford. For it was just then that a woman's voice, soft, cold, precise, broke into the conversation.

'It is not true,' it said.

Startled, the sergeant looked up. Toby turned round. George, who had sat down on a chair in a far corner, rose to his feet with diffident courtesy. In the doorway stood a very small old woman. She wore an old-fashioned seal-skin coat and a felt hat that looked as if she generally kept in rolled up in a pocket and only put it on in the rain. Blue eyes burnt out of a deeply wrinkled but delicate face.

'It is not true,' she said. 'Show him to me. I know it is not true.'

Quietly Toby stepped back beside George. The sergeant stood up, hanging up the receiver blunderingly so that it made a noisy tinkling.

'I'm sorry, your ladyship . . .'

'No, no, it's my husband who should be sorry. You are not at all to blame, Eggbear—why should you be? It happens that I know it cannot be true. But I wish to see him and to assure you, looking at him, that this poor man is not my son. You would not doubt me in those circumstances?'

The sergeant had reddened. He came round from behind his table. 'But, your ladyship, Sir Joseph—'

'I've been speaking to Sir Joseph.' She smiled. She sat down on the chair that the sergeant placed for her, and unbuttoned her seal-skin coat. The dress she was wearing inside it was of a green, coarsely handwoven material, with odd little pieces of embroidery that looked as if they had been saved off a dozen different dresses stitched on to it. She wore a silver chain from which hung various pieces of cornelian, moss-agate, topaz and amber, which suggested that she collected her jewellery by walking round our shores.

'I met Sir Joseph at the end of the village.' Her voice, though quiet and gentle had still that cold, even sound. There was a remoteness, too, about the sweet smile with which she went on looking at the sergeant. She seemed to form both smile and words with a deliberateness that made them strangely unliving. 'I had followed him, you see, as soon as I learnt what it was that had brought him so suddenly to Chovey. He didn't wish me to know, of course, but as he always refuses to answer a telephone himself—I don't blame him for that, you know, I feel just the same way about it—anyway, it meant, you see, that Harvey, who's really *very* good with the telephone, really very clever with it indeed, Harvey was able to tell me why Sir Joseph had suddenly ordered out the car to go into Chovey. So I followed immediately. Harvey drove me—he's such a capable man, though Sir Joseph says he drives recklessly, but there I don't agree with him; I always feel quite safe with Harvey. Well, at the end of the village we met the other car, and my husband told me that he had just been telling you that this poor dead man is our son Shelley. Oh, Eggbear, I feel so ashamed of his having done such a thing, putting you in this *dreadfully* awkward position. I don't know how he *could.*'

'But, your ladyship,' said Eggbear confusedly, 'here's his passport, found in the jacket he left—'

She scarcely looked at it. Her soft voice went on: 'Of course it may have been a genuine mistake. I understand the man's face has been very much damaged. But it isn't only by his face that one recognizes one's son. Indeed no.'

'But here's his photograph, and even I can recognize that,' the sergeant was expostulating, but again the gentle voice defeated him:

'My husband is a strange man, Eggbear. An earnest and sincere man in many ways, but in this matter I think you would be wise to trust me rather than him. Now please will you take me to where I can look at this poor, poor fellow. You mustn't think it'll upset me just because I'm a woman. I'm not that sort of person; I shall be just as strong as my husband. And what I tell you will undoubtedly be more reliable.'

The sergeant made a slight, helpless gesture. His eyes,

meeting Toby's for a moment, signalled bewildered resignation. He led Lady Maxwell out.

It was as she was going that she seemed, for the first time to notice Toby. She smiled at him and bowed. There was the graciousness about her of one who, accustomed to being recognized wherever she goes, is anxious to avoid offending anyone by her lack of recognition.

Toby hesitated for an instant, looking about her. Then, with swift steps, he followed. George loitered along after him.

The body was in an outhouse at the back of the police station. With small, pattering steps, Lady Maxwell advanced. There was a glitter in her eyes and her head was poked forward in curious, eager interest; only her lips, the sunken lips of age, worked against one another nervously.

For a full minute she stood there, saying nothing. She had coughed faintly on entering, as if she were drawing the attention of the dead man to her intrusion. Now she murmured: 'How could he, oh, how could he?'

Eggbear looked round at Toby and gave a surreptitious tap on his forehead. But Toby was absorbed in watching Lady Maxwell.

Taking a step forward, she touched one of the dead man's hands.

'Of course,' she said, 'I knew it couldn't be, but Joseph having made this ridiculous mistake, I had to come here and *show* you. You'll believe, won't you, that a mother couldn't be mistaken about her son?'

The sergeant replied with an unintelligible monosyllable.

'I've been feeling so sorry for poor Mrs Milne,' she went on. 'I admire Mrs Milne very much. So independent, so—so indomitable, I feel. And I'm so sorry for this poor fellow and for his friends or relatives, whoever they turn out to be. So sad and so unnecessary, a death of this kind.

Well, thank you, Eggbear, I think I'll go home now.'

Her voice was still tranquil. But in going she caught for a moment at the doorpost, clutching it, her knuckles standing out like white pebbles on the shrivelled brown of her hand. The next moment she was walking on. She bowed again to Toby and George, thanked the sergeant, and pattered out to her car.

The sergeant saw her out to it. He saw Harvey, the manservant from Chovey Place, tuck her into it with plenty of rugs. She thanked Harvey for everything he did for her, and again thanked the sergeant. Returning into the police station, he growled: 'Now what the hell d'you make of that?'

'Why, marriage is a very beautiful thing, Sam,' Toby replied. 'Maternity too, of course, but more particularly marriage.'

'Poor woman,' said Eggbear sombrely.

'Oh, I don't know about that. She seemed quite happy.'

'Can't bear to face the truth, that's how 'tis. And think o' that husband o' hers lettin' her come here by herself . . .'

'I mentioned the occasional beauty of marriage,' said Toby.

Eggbear grunted. At that moment the telephone started ringing. He reached out for it. Putting it down again after a minute of conversation, he looked gravely into Toby's face.

'This,' he said, 'is the darndest accident I ever had to do with.'

'What's got unhooked now?'

'That suitcase. 'Twas in the Wallaford station cloakroom all right, deposited there on Tuesday mornin'. A leather suitcase with the initials SM. But 'twas collected yesterday mornin'.' He frowned, running the end of his pencil up and down the corrugations on his forehead, as if he were playing the xylophone. 'Collected,' he added, 'by a tall, dark man with glasses.'

*

The inquest was held that afternoon in the Ring of Bells.

The evidence of Mrs Quantick from Wallaford, of the passport and of Sir Joseph Maxwell was accepted. The body was held to be that of Shelley Maxwell. Sir Joseph was granted a burial certificate.

But in view of the fact that the driver of the sports car that had passed Mrs Milne's, who might prove to have been a witness of the accident itself, or at least to have seen Shelley Maxwell alive, had not yet come forward, the police asked for an adjournment.

CHAPTER 6

If a man stays a night at an hotel, or even two nights, if he has not sent the address of this hotel to any of his acquantances or creditors, if, in fact, he has barely given himself time to realize that he is stopping there, he does not expect any post.

Yet on Friday morning there was a letter for Toby Dyke.

He woke up to see it a few inches in front of his nose. Through the clouds of drowsiness and through his resentment at the fact that someone, contrary to instructions, must have wakened him, he saw an oblong of white with his own name written on it in block capitals.

'TOBY DYKE ESQ. THE RING OF BELLS. CHOVEY.'

He shut his eyes. But as soon as he did so he felt a hand on his shoulder.

He gave an impatient lurch in the bed. However, as someone was sitting on its edge, the space for lurching in was uncomfortably constricted. He opened his eyes again and saw the letter still being held before him, as, were he thought to be probably dead, a mirror might be held to see if his breath would stain it.

'What the hell is it?' he asked in thick and sullen tones.

'It's the post,' said George patiently.

'Can't be. The post doesn't come till eight-thirty. Never does, anywhere.'

'Hear that?' said George. 'It's ten o'clock striking.'

Toby edged a hand from under the bedclothes and took the letter.

'You know, Tobe, what you ought to do when you wake up is eat barley-sugar,' said George. 'It'd make you feel better.'

'Would it?'

'Sure. I knew a bloke one could hardly tell apart from you up to breakfast-time. He got different later on—he was a dancing instructor. But he hadn't enough sugar in his blood, and the morning's the time when that shows. You want to get a jar of barley-sugar, or maybe chocolate biscuits—'

'George,' said Toby, who was sitting up, 'this is a pretty queer letter.'

'Well, I thought—' George was beginning.

'Take a look at it,' said Toby, and thrust the single sheet of paper towards him.

George took it. But he only glanced at it, then turned his eyes sideways into a corner of the room.

'As a matter of *absolute* fact,' he said in an embarrassed voice, 'I've read it.'

One of Toby's black eyebrows hooked itself up. 'When?'

'Well, you were so late coming down,' said George, 'and there it sat, looking so damn queer . . .'

'But it was stuck up,' said Toby.

George put a hand in a pocket and brought out a little tube of seccotine. 'And you'd never notice the smell, Tobe. I would, but you wouldn't.'

Toby grunted. 'Well, it's queer all right. Or just plain

nasty.' He took the letter back from George and looked it over once more.

It was a sheet of cheap, lined paper, the kind that is advertised nowadays as suitable for airmail. It had no address, no signature. Letters cut from a newspaper and pasted on to the paper composed its message, which ran: 'YOU WERE LOOKING FOR A BOTTLE WEREN'T YOU? WHAT ABOUT THE FLASK IN MRS MILNE'S CAR?'

'Been thinking it over, George?' said Toby.

George nodded.

'Well, I'm having my breakfast before I give it any careful thought. Here, get off my bed; that's the side I get out.'

George got up and withdrew against the wall. 'Tobe,' he said earnestly, 'I'd never have opened it if it had been an ordinary letter. But it was the knowing you hadn't given the address to anyone, and the block letters—they've been done with a ruler and a hard pencil—'

'Have they, by God?' Toby, half out of bed, paused and picked the envelope off the eiderdown. 'Careful beggar. Posted here in Chovey. Well, we'll take it along to the sergeant to help cheer him up. You go and tell them I'll want my eggs and bacon in ten minutes.'

He lit himself another cigarette, then started dressing.

About an hour and a half later, when Toby handed the anonymous letter over to Sergeant Eggbear, the symptoms of cheerfulness that it produced in him were a sinking of his heavy chin, a lowering of his eyebrows and a hissing sound through his teeth.

'"You were looking for a bottle weren't you? What about the flask in Mrs Milne's car?" Damn them, this is just the sort o' thing that would start up, now 'tis known as the fellow was Bish Maxwell. Someone tryin' to make trouble between Maxwells and Mrs Milne. 'You were looking for a—"' He looked up suddenly at Toby. 'When were *you* lookin' for a bottle?'

Toby shrugged his shoulders. 'Whom did your constable tell about it?'

'Yes, might've been that way. Cecil—where's Cecil? Who's the lad been talkin' to?'

'What I'd like to know,' said Toby, 'is who's got a grudge against your Mrs Milne. What I mean is, do you feel like making guesses about who sent this, or do you have to start from the bottom?'

But the sergeant preferred to settle one thing at a time, and it was not until he had questioned Leat and had received the answer that he had happened to mention the co-operation of Toby Dyke and his friend in the bottle-hunt to quite a number of people, that Toby's question had its turn.

'Toby,' said the sergeant then, 'I'm goin to tell you the whole thing, just as it happened. 'Tis botherin' me.' And he went over the story, from the time that Mrs Milne had hurried, white-faced, into the police station, until the present. Toby had already heard most of it, but there were some details in it, such as a description of Leat's visit to the major, that were new.

Toby nodded at each slight interval in the story, but at the end of it he said: 'Yes, Sam, but what you haven't given me is the background. You've left out the social side of it. These people, the Maxwells, Mrs Milne, what are they like? What's their relation to one another?'

Eggbear played the xylophone up and down his forehead. He looked uncomfortable and unwilling to say anything. All at once, with a charging rush of words, he started: 'You know how 'tis in this kind o' place, Toby—all talk, everywhere you go, naught but talk. I was out in my garden this mornin' lookin' if there was some violets for my missis to take to her mother today over to Purbrook. What with the frost there wasn't any, though the bed's full o' buds. But what I mean to say is, if you was to go out in the street and ask the first person you see what Sergeant Eggbear was doin' at half-past seven this mornin', he'd answer on the nail: ''Pickin' violets.'' And if you was to ask him what he knew about Maxwells and Milnes he'd answer just as fast, and all as if he'd seen it with his own eyes. Well, maybe *some* of what he told you might be true . . .'

'Yes, yes,' said Toby, 'but that's what I want. Some of the scandal of the neighbourhood. Something to make me take an interest.'

George gave a chuckle.

'Well, go on, Sam,' said Toby.

But the sergeant was still hesitant. It was rumoured, he said, that Sir Joseph and Mrs Milne were not at all friendly. But she was dining up to the Place the other night, so what did you make of that? It was rumoured that Sir Joseph and Lady Maxwell quarrelled about Mrs Milne; it was rumoured that Sir Joseph and his brother, the major, quarrelled about her too; it was rumoured that Daphne Milne was always quarrelling with her mother, in fact had had a quarrel with her and gone off to London only last week, and that was supposed to be about Adrian Laws—but weren't Mrs Milne and young Laws in the Ring of Bells the other night, quite friendly like? And then, Mrs Milne wasn't what you'd call good at keeping her servants . . .

Toby sat on a corner of the table, frowning. 'Not,' he said, his slanting, dark eyes glowering at the anonymous message, 'a very popular lady. At any rate, her popularity with some people only increases her unpopularity with others. That's her sort. I think, Sam, George and I are going along to have a chat with her about this letter.' And with a swinging movement of his long legs he was off the table and pulling George towards the door.

But his haste did not succeed in leaving Sergeant Eggbear behind them. If Mrs Milne was to be interviewed about the letter it was only proper, the sergeant explained with unusually dour stubbornness, that he should be in charge. It was in his Austin Seven, some minutes later, that the three of them approached The Laurels.

They were shown by Cecil Leat's cousin Ruby into Mrs Milne's green-and-grey drawing-room.

Coming up the drive, standing on the doorstep, crossing the polished parquet of the hall, they had heard a piano. Chopin, but now from this waltz and now from that study —all of it, however, of the easier kind. It was impatient, muddled playing, and not particularly musical. As Ruby opened the drawing-room door it stopped abruptly.

A girl seated at the piano looked over her shoulder at them, then stood up.

She was a girl of slim hips and long, slim legs, waving fair hair and eyes as remarkably blue as a cynodendron. Skin of a dazzling freshness and fairness drew attention from the fact that her features were not distinguished. There was, in the terms of the cosmetic advertisements, a blooming naturalness about her. That is to say, there was only a very little powder on her face, her lipstick was only a shade pinker and brighter than her lips themselves would have been, and her hair appeared as if the wind had been at it—a cunning wind, however, with Bond Street experience behind it. She wore slim, well-tailored tweeds and golf shoes and a check blouse with a childish-looking little round collar and a big bow at her neck.

One hand went nervously to this bow, as she stood there, to tug at an end of it.

'Good morning,' she said, with a husky softness that had the effect of an unexpected shyness. Her glance went over the three of them, then came to rest on Toby.

'Mornin', Miss Milne,' said Eggbear. 'I'd heard you was up to London. Did you have a nice time?'

'I was only up for a day or two,' she answered, still looking at the dark and somewhat striking face behind the sergeant, 'shopping and so on. I—I didn't do much exciting.'

'You're mother's in, I'm told.'

'Y-yes, I'll go and . . . I don't expect she'll . . . Do sit down, Sergeant Eggbear; I'll see if . . .' And she made a dive for the door. But even then her eyes came round once more to gaze into Toby's. As she pulled the door shut behind her Toby let out the breath he had been holding.

'My God, what a glorious girl!'

'Yes,' said Eggbear, 'she's pretty.'

Toby laughed derisively. 'Pretty! But what a pity, Sam, that such a gorgeous creature should be so frightened.'

'Ah, that don't mean anythin'. She always was a shy sort of girl.'

Again a knowledgeable laugh answered him. 'My good Sam, that shyness is only a part of her picture of herself. But her eyes, her eyes! That wasn't shyness, that wasn't dewy wood-fairyness, that was fear.'

This time the sergeant chose to laugh.

'Maybe,' said George, 'the sergeant don't know what fear looks like in the eyes of a beautiful girl, like you do, Tobe.'

With a sharp frown of suspicion Toby looked round at him. But George was gazing at his own reflection in the gold-framed, convex mirror that hung above the fireplace. From the way he was bulging his eyes and mouthing, it looked as if he must be trying to catch up with the distortion of the reflection.

'Stop that, George, she's coming!' Toby turned quickly to the door.

Mrs Milne, in her greeting, was gravely inquiring. She seemed to assume that the sergeant would not have called upon her with his friend unless the matter were of some importance. She said: 'Good morning, Mr Dyke,' without waiting for Toby to be introduced to her, and when they were all seated, she in a deep easy chair, she said: 'I've been half-expecting you, Sergeant. I've been having a feeling that this thing wasn't at an end.' On the arms of the chair her hands, with their flashing rings, lay with a limpness unlike the tension of her neck and shoulders.

Eggbear sat on the edge of one of the easy chairs, his knees together, his feet side by side. 'This morning, ma'am,' he said, 'my friend, Mr Dyke, received a letter. As he had not given his address to anyone he was naturally surprised. As it concerns you . . .' He reached out his hand for the letter which Toby had taken from his pocket. 'Here it is, ma'am. We thought you belonged to take a look at it.'

She took the letter. There was no change on her face as she read it, but from the length of time she looked at it she must have read it over several times before she spoke.

'Am I right,' she said then, looking at Toby, 'that the implication of this letter is that I murdered Shelley Maxwell?'

'I shouldn't be surprised,' said Toby.

'He was dead drunk, wasn't he? His stomach was swimming in whisky. That meant that he must have drunk it a very few minutes before he was killed. But you searched, didn't you—' she still had her steady gaze on Toby—'and couldn't find anything that might have contained the whisky?'

'Inference,' said Toby, 'someone removed it.'

'Yes,' she said, 'and suppose it was I who removed it. And not only removed it, but gave it to him in the first place. The inference then is that he was not lying in the road when I first encountered him. Probably he was standing up. Probably I talked to him. So when I drove my car over his head I must have known that he was there . . .'

Toby was staring fascinated at the stillness of her ringed hands. 'D'you know,' he remarked, 'you're about the most controlled woman I've ever run into.'

She started then, and her hands came quickly together. Toby smiled at her with irony.

'Do you,' he said, 'happen to keep a flask in your car?'

'Yes, I do.'

'Could you say off-hand whether it's full or empty at the moment?'

'No, I haven't the slightest idea. I—' She hesitated and her eyes suddenly looked unguarded and afraid. 'It must be full, I think. There was that big accident last December at the railway crossing on the Plymouth road. You remember—' she turned for a moment to the sergeant—'I came up just after it happened. I had my flask out then, giving some whisky to the man who wasn't killed. I *think* I filled it up again afterwards—yes, I did, I know I did—the same evening. But I haven't thought about it since.'

'You're sure about that?' said Toby.

'Y-yes, sure.'

'Then wouldn't it be a good idea,' said Toby, 'to show it to the sergeant now?'

She got to her feet. 'Come along.'

As they came out into the hall there was the sound of footsteps on the landing overhead and then on the stairs, and Daphne Milne appeared round the bend in the staircase. She stood still as soon as she saw them, looking first at her mother, but then, as if she could not help herself, let her big eyes gaze into Toby's. For a moment he paused before her, but a pressure in the small of his back from George sent him on after Mrs Milne. He followed her down a short passage and out through glass doors at the end of it on to the gravel drive, which, sweeping round the house, came to an end at a large, stone garage.

The garage doors were open. As they approached a man came out and went down a path towards the kitchen garden.

'Chauffeur?' said Toby.

'Well, gardener really,' said Mrs Milne, 'but he does drive me sometimes and he looks after the car. Now that—' and she pointed— 'is where the flask is. Look for yourselves.'

Toby took a step forward. But with his hand on the door of the car he stopped. 'I've a feeling,' he said, 'that you think we may be backing this anonymous letter.'

She shrugged her shoulders. 'No, I don't know that I do. I appreciate your bringing it to me. Please go on.'

Toby leant in through the door of the saloon and felt round in the pigeon-hole on the dashboard. Behind some fur gloves, some maps and sun-glasses, he found a flask. It was a glass flask, its base fitting into a silver cup. He held it up. It was full within about an inch of the stopper.

Mrs Milne saw it with a crooked smile. As Toby handed it to the sergeant she said: 'I think it would have to be emptier than that to meet the case, wouldn't it?'

'Yes, that it would,' he said. ' 'Tis the way with these sorts o' letters, you don't expect to find anythin' behind'n.'' He held the flask out for Toby to replace, but it was George who took it from him, replacing it himself. 'Can you give us any pointer at who might have written the letter?' Eggbear went on.

'No, nothing with any foundation. There's nothing to go on, is there? And one may know that a person has a grudge against one—' She stopped. Then she smiled oddly and went on: 'One may know that a person has a grudge against one without believing for a moment that it'd come to anonymous letter-writing. I should think this probably comes from some malicious person I've never even heard of. After all, the inquest made quite public the importance of a bottle or flask. And now'—they had arrived once more at the glass doors that led into the house—'I was in the middle of some work when you arrived. If you don't mind . . .' And the glass doors closed behind her.

They stood there for a moment, looking at the closed doors. Toby cocked an eyebrow at the sergeant.

'Work?' he said. 'What sort of work'd that be?'

Eggbear shook his head.

'Washing stockings, maybe,' George suggested.

'Don't be a damn fool,' said Toby, and spinning suddenly on his heel, set off down the drive.

He walked in frowning silence. Eggbear and George walked a little way behind him, the space between Toby and the two of them steadily lengthening as Toby's impatient strides outdistanced theirs. Near the gate he halted abruptly and waited for them to catch up.

'Anyway,' he said, 'where does her money come from?'

'Why, from her husband, I reckon,' said Eggbear.

'What was he?'

'Couldn't say. Couldn't so much as say when he died. She was a widow when she come to live here.'

Toby nodded and pushed open the gate.

It was George who, as they arrived beside the sergeant's car, said that he wanted to go for a walk to get up his appetite for dinner. He looked down at the ground as he said it and drew circles on the gravel with the point of his shoe. Toby, still frowning, gave him a stare. George did not look up, but carefully divided one of the circles he had drawn into segments.

Toby let his hand drop from the door of the car. 'All right,' he said, 'I'll come too. See you later, Sam.'

Looking Napoleonic in his Austin Seven, Eggbear drove off alone.

They strolled a little way down the road. George was quietly whistling.

'Well, George, what's on your mind?'

George pulled a piece of grass out of the hedge and stuck it between his teeth. 'That flask.'

'What about it?'

'I gave it a smell as I was putting it back.'

'And—'

'It smelt of whisky.'

Toby gave a bark of laughter. But it broke off in the middle. 'Did it, by God?' His face looked suddenly eager. 'You're sure of it? No imagination? Whisky was probably the uppermost thought in your mind. It was in mine.'

George shook his head. 'Smelt quite strong,' he said, tugging at the piece of grass in his mouth.

Toby laughed again with a sharp ring of pleasure. 'And it's how long ago she said she had it filled last? After the big accident she talked about. Last December. Come on, George, we're going back.'

But George shook his head again, his jaws working slowly as he muched at the grass. 'Don't necessarily mean a thing, Tobe. You've got to remember the gardener.'

'It's the gardener I want.'

'Oh!' George threw the grass into the ditch, picked another piece and started towards The Laurels.

This time they did not go immediately to the front gate, but skirting along the laurel hedge, the garden's high, dark rampart, searched for some other entrance, which, if it existed, might let them into the kitchen garden without their being forced to pass under the windows of the house.

Luckily it was there, a narrow, wooden gate. It was high; Toby could only just see over it; also it turned out to be padlocked. But Toby could see the gardener, not twenty yards away, forking a patch of soil, his back to the gate.

Toby called.

He called three times before the man took any notice. Then all he did was to pause in his digging and cock his head slightly as if he thought he had heard an unaccustomed noise.

'Over here,' called Toby.

The man looked round then, saw him at last and came

towards him. He walked with the slow steps of one who is used to a load of soil on his boots. He was a square, stolid man with a brown face and very little hair; there were deep wrinkles round his eyes and line after line of them scored across his high bald forehead. His lips had the fallen-in look of too few teeth, and indeed, as they parted, they revealed only three or four whitish spikes sticking down from his gum.

'Mornin',' he said, ' 'tis a fine day. Better'n yesterday. Better'n this time last year.'

Toby addressed him in the loud voice one uses to the deaf. 'Good morning. Do you happen to remember seeing us a short while ago with Sergeant Eggbear?'

The man looked at him in a puzzled way. Toby repeated it in a louder voice. The man shook his head.

' 'E don't require to talk so loud,' he said. 'I ain't deaf. I was thinkin'.'

'Sorry,' said Toby. 'Well, do you remember—?'

'Ah, I remembers. But 'twas my teeth I was a-thinkin' about. There's a hole in this one up here that hurts terrible the moment I stop workin'. 'Tis the circulation, I reckon. Minute ago I wasn't givin' it a thought, but then you calls me and I stops and stands up and looks around, and the old devil starts up as if he was diggin' in my head with a red-hot pitchfork.'

'Why don't you get it seen to?' said Toby.

'Ah,' said the man, 'that's what the lady says. Mrs Milne, her says: "Albert," her says, "you belong to go and have it seen to, that tooth o' yours." "Ma'am," I says, "when I had more teeth in my head than I have, I was always a-goin' to the dentist. Went to him for a pastime, I did. And what did he do? Stopped up the holes in'n, and when the stoppin' come out he stopped'n up again. Well," I says, "I reckon that ain't good enough. Now I keeps my teeth the way they are until I can't stand'n no more, and then I has'n out. No, ma'am," I says, "I don't hold with dentists."'

'Well, I was just going to ask you—'

But sticking his fork into the ground and leaning upon it, Albert went on: 'Mrs Milne, her says: "But I'll pay for it myself, Albert," her says. "For the sake of your health, that's why. And you belong to have some false teeth in, you can't be chewin' your food proper." "Thankin' you, ma'am," I says, "but—"'

In a clear voice, which he had slightly raised again, Toby struck in: 'Ever tried whisky for your toothache, Albert?'

Staring at the two heads that looked at him over the top of the gate, Albert fell silent. He pulled his fork out of the ground, looked down for a moment at the worn prongs, then, as he thrust it into the earth once more, looked back at his questioner.

'Well,' he said, 'I have.'

'Ah,' said Toby, 'when?'

'I thought,' said Albert, 'you and Eggbear was up here because of the accident.'

'That's right,' said Toby.

'Then—'

'Just you tell me,' said Toby, 'when you had a swig at that whisky in the car. Mrs Milne won't hear of it.'

Albert eyed him speculatively, then answered in a fatalistic voice: 'All right, then. This mornin'.'

Toby looked startled. 'But look here,' he said, 'this morning that flask ought to have been empty.'

Albert nodded. 'I had'n filled. Took it round and got Ruby to fill'n.'

Toby gave a bark of triumph. 'It *was* empty!'

'Aye,' said Albert, 'and how it come to be I couldn't say. 'Twas more'n half full Tuesday.'

'Oh, you had a spot on Tuesday too?'

'Aye, 'twas Tuesday I come over queer—a touch o' the influenza, I reckon—I come over queer with pains in my body and a kind o' faintness, and I thinks to myself: 'There's whisky in that car, and the lady'd be the last to begrudge it you.' So I take a drop, and that leaves the flask a bit over half full, like I was sayin'. Then I go home to bed, and stay in bed all Wednesday. Yesterday I get up for my dinner, but I stay in by the fire and listen to the wireless, and then today I'm back at work. I've a very sound constitution; illness don't keep me down long. But as I was tellin' you—'

'Hi, hi!' said George suddenly, his blue eyes excited. 'You weren't at work yesterday?'

Albert shook his head.

'Mrs Milne,' said George, 'is she much of a gardener?'

Albert laughed derisively, and George subsided out of sight behind the gate.

'And you say,' said Toby, 'that the flask was empty this morning?'

'That's right,' said Albert. 'Half full Tuesday, and empty this mornin'. I was surprised, but when I heard o' the accident I allowed as 'twas somethin' to do with that.'

'It was,' said Toby. 'Thank you.'

Albert replied that he was welcome, and, pulling up his fork once more, returned with those weighted steps of his to the patch of soil he had been digging.

Toby looked down at George, who now was squatting at the foot of the hedge. He had his elbows on his knees, his plump face held in his hands.

'George,' he said, 'what made you ask if Mrs Milne was a gardener?'

George went on staring straight ahead of him. 'When you were taking a sleep after your dinner yesterday afternoon,' he said, 'before the inquest, I went for a walk.'

'You're doing an awful lot of walking, George.'

'Yes,' said George. 'Well, I came along here. Someone was doing a bit of gardening—that's to say, someone was making a bonfire. I smelt it.'

'Well, what about it?'

George shrugged his shoulders. 'Don't know. What about that flask? Why were you so sure it'd be empty this morning?'

'Just a guess,' said Toby, 'though I felt fairly sure that whoever sent that letter knew that the flask was empty. And since it *was*—George, there *is* something in all this. I don't know what it is, but it's there. If that flask had been full, or rather, if it'd been the same as our Albert left it on Tuesday, that letter wouldn't have meant a thing. But as it is . . .'

George heaved himself on to his feet. 'Well, speaking for myself and myself alone,' he said, 'I'd like my dinner. But I don't suppose that's in your reckoning yet.'

'Why not?' said Toby. 'I'm as hungry as you are. Come on, we'll be getting back.'

'Eh?' said Geroge. 'D'you mean to say you're going to let that chap's story go uncorroborated?'

Unwillingly Toby replied: 'Well, I suppose while we're at it . . .'

'That's right,' said George. 'Here, we can get through the hedge. Albert's just gone in to dinner. You let me go ahead, then you won't tear your clothes.'

'No,' said Mrs Milne's cook at the back door, 'we don't want anything.'

But from behind her Ruby, the parlourmaid, had seen the two men.

'Sh, Martha,' she said, 'they'm the two gentlemen who come up with Sergeant Eggbear this mornin'.'

At once the hard, square face of the woman before them took on a look of eagerness. She was short, broad and vigorous, with thick, muscular arms and hands which, reddened, scrubbed and cracked, seemed to clench themselves into fists the moment they had nothing to do. Her age might be forty or forty-five. She had shrewd eyes and a confident mouth.

'Ah,' she said, that eagerness on her face adding an intimidating quality to her grim features, 'you want to know what I know. Well, I don't mind telling you. It's time someone spoke the truth. And you'll get nothing but the truth from me. Everyone knows that. I speak the truth and nothing but the truth—always, so help me God.'

'Fine,' said Toby. 'Now there's a question—'

'Ask anyone you like, that's what they'll tell you,' she swept on before he could get any further. 'Folk don't always like it—oh no, I know the sort of things they say of me when I'm not there. But it's not for their sakes I do it, but for the sake of the Grace Divine, which will encompass me if I have faith and walk in the way of righteousness—yea, even me, miserable sinner that I am. So you see, young man, you've come to the right place. No lies for me, no mincing matters. I'll tell you what I know about that woman, under whose roof I'd be shamed to have you find me if it weren't that I scorn to break a contract. No, I don't leave even such a house as this without giving full notice and working as well up to the last day as I did at the first. No one shall have cause to blame *me* for my conduct, and what's more—'

Toby spoke in a loud voice, trying to batter hers down: 'There's just one specific question I want answered.'

She nodded curtly, and went straight on: 'This is a house of corruption. There's no vice you won't find here—drunkenness and Sabbath-breaking, and all kinds of lewdness. Ah, it's time it was looked into, that it is. Her speech is blasphemous; she talks blasphemies aloud to herself even when there's no one there to hear her! And then that accident of hers! Says it wasn't her fault, says the man was drunk. You believe me, it was *her* who was drunk! Who'd ever believe her, I'd like to know, if she hadn't the money she's got?'

'There's one specific—' Toby began again, but again it was lost.

'Listen,' she said, 'you can believe *me*. I'm not rich, I can't twist others to my purposes, I've nothing to gain or lose. I tell the truth fearlessly and face the consequences. You believe I tell the truth, don't you?'

'Yes, if you like, but—'

'Then I tell you, you can believe me, that woman's doing something—' Suddenly Martha's tense face reddened. She looked down at the ground and finished in a much less certain voice: 'She's doing something she ought not.'

'And that,' said Toby sternly, 'is what you call not mincing matters.'

She glanced up at him with an almost abashed expression. One of her fists unclenched themselves; her fingers started tweaking the edge of her apron. 'I can't bring myself to say it,' she said. 'I'm not used to speaking such words. I meant to denounce her to the law, but I can't take such vileness on my tongue. I can't—' She stopped abruptly, gaping at him in a strained and foolish way, almost as if she might burst into tears, turned from him and stumbled back into the kitchen.

Ruby came quickly to the door, meaning to shut them out.

Toby put a hand on her wrist.

'Come out here a moment,' he said, and drew her out on to the doorstep. 'I want a question answered. Did Albert, the gardener, bring a flask to you this morning to be filled up?'

Her chin hanging, her eyes bulging, Ruby nodded.

'Was it empty, half-empty, or what?'

'Not a drop in it!' Ruby gasped at him.

He let her go. But then he stopped her again. 'You couldn't take that particular vileness on your own tongue, I suppose, and tell me what cook thinks our Mrs Milne has been up to?'

'I don't know, indeed I don't. She always talks that

way,' said Ruby. 'She never says straight out what 'tis.'

'Can't you guess?' said Toby.

Ruby shook her head with a kind of desperation.

'Hm, can't you! Look here, how long ago did it start?'

'What?' bleated Ruby.

'This nameless evil. When did cook start slinging the mud in that particular direction?'

'I don't know, oh, I don't know . . . Yes, I do, though. 'Twas the evening Martha's sister was here—Martha's sister in to Purbrook, Mrs Langman. She come to spend the day here with Martha, and the same evening Martha give in her notice. So maybe 'twas something Mrs Langman told her.'

Toby brought an old envelope and a stub of pencil out of his pocket. 'I think I'll have Mrs Langman's address. D'you know it?'

Ruby nodded, but said: 'Maybe I don't belong to give it you. Maybe Martha wouldn't like it.'

'Come on,' said Toby, 'you give it me. Mrs Langman . . .?' He wrote that much and waited.

But Ruby only stared at him with apprehension on her round face.

'Martha don't mean any harm,' she said.

'I know, I know; someone put her in a dark cupboard when she was young. But if you start up slanders you must expect to have them substantiated. Mrs Langman . . .?'

This time, with a nervous glance behind her, Ruby gave the address. Toby wrote, and returned envelope and pencil to his pocket. He thanked Ruby, and Ruby, with an ear still for any sounds from within, muttered thanks for his shilling. He set off across the kitchen garden by the way that he and George had come.

In the road, on their way back to Chovey, George said to him: 'How did you know, Tobe?'

Toby was striding fast, his dark face grim with ideas.

'What?' he asked, but the word had an inattentive sound.

'About her having been put in a dark cupboard.'

Toby snorted and strode on.

Forced into trotting, George continued: 'Well, what do you think it is?'

'What?' Toby repeated with irritation.

'This sin.'

'Sexual, of course.'

'Yes, I thought so too,' said George.

'Brilliant of you.'

'Well, who d'you think it is?'

'Who what is? For the Lord's sake, say it all in one!'

'Her lover, of course.'

'The most probable on the scene is Maxwell, isn't it?'

'What, the chap she done in?'

'Oh, my God—no, the major.'

'Oh,' said George, and seeming to have no other questions to ask, no longer troubled to keep up.

Toby, forging ahead, was seated at his table in the coffee-room of the Ring of Bells before George was even in sight of the inn.

It was when they were both sitting in a fully occupied silence over the Irish stew that had been warmed up for them by an even-tempered cook, that Toby remarked: 'You know, George, it might have been the Milne girl.'

'Eh?' said George.

'The one who was gardening on Thursday afternoon. The one who lit the bonfire.'

George shook his head. 'Notice her hands? Never done a tougher job than a manicure. No,' he went on as Toby frowned at him doubtingly, 'you needn't put it on, Tobe; I know you didn't notice them. She took darn good care that you'd only notice her eyes.'

CHAPTER 7

Chovey is built mostly along one straight road. It swells slightly about the middle, where the church, the eighteenth-century almshouses, the school and a number of old cottages cluster together. It has, in fact, somewhat the formation of a breeding worm.

From the grey, stone solidity of The Laurels at one end to a nine months old bungalow at the other, it stretches about three quarters of a mile. There are several hundred yards of bungalows. They are all built of a hard-looking, white brick that never mellows, have two rooms, kitchen, bathroom and indoor sanitation, and steeply pitched roofs of pink asbestos tiles. In one of these, in pride and moderate comfort, lived Sergeant and Mrs Eggbear.

That evening Toby and George ate their supper in its sitting-room. They ate cold chicken, apple pie and Devonshire cream, trifle with almonds and more Devonshire cream on top, and biscuits and cheese. Mrs Eggbear apologized; she said that Friday was her day for visiting her mother in Purbrook, so she had not had time to get them a proper meal.

When she had cleared away the supper she brought in tea.

Toby, full of food and stretched out almost at full length in a cretonne-covered chair, his cup and saucer resting against his chest, remarked presently, 'Somebody is trying to pull me into stirring up some local slime, Sam. Who is it?'

The sergeant dropped another lump of sugar into his tea. 'There's nothin' to go on,' he said. 'You take my word for it, you won't find out anythin'. You won't find out anythin' unless some more letters come. Then maybe you'll be able to add one thing and another and get an answer. But that letter on its own don't give anythin' away.'

'It gives away one thing,' said Toby, sipping tea, 'no, two.'

'What's that?' said Eggbear.

'One: the writer's someone who knew the flask was there—'

'Might be almost anyone. The time of the big accident there was a whole crowd saw Mrs Milne give a drink to the man who'd passed out.'

'Well then, two: the writer's someone who knew that the flask was empty on Tuesday night—or at least some time between Tuesday and today.'

'Yes, well?' said Eggbear.

'How many people are there,' said Toby, 'who stand a chance of being able to get a look inside Mrs Milne's car?'

The sergeant did a little meditative nodding to show that he had comprehended.

Mrs Eggbear suggested: 'Would you like a pencil and paper?'

'I think I've got most of them in my head already,' said Toby. 'There's Mrs Milne herself and her daughter. There's the cook, and the maid, and the gardener. There's that young chap, Laws. There's the major. Those two—Laws and Maxwell, I mean—came down to the Ring of Bells on Wednesday evening in Mrs Milne's car. They may actually never have had a moment to themselves in the car, still, one's got to count them in. And then there are the two old Maxwells.'

'Eh?' said Eggbear.

'The other three had been up to Chovey Place for dinner, hadn't they? The car must have been standing about somewhere up there—outside the door, or in a garage. And it probably wasn't locked. Or would one lock one's car when one went to visit the Maxwells?'

Mrs Eggbear tittered.

George observed: 'But at that rate, Tobe, you'll have to count in all the Maxwell servants.'

An impatient frown gathered above Toby's beak of a nose. But the sergeant looked round at George. Pink in the face from the heat of the fire, he was sitting on a sort of tuffet of coloured leather and beads.

'That's right!' said Eggbear, and on a note of rising enthusiasm: 'That's right! I believe you've hit somethin', Mr—excuse me, but what *is* your name? Reckon I've never heard it.'

'Posslethwaite,' said George.

'Mr Posslethwaite. 'Twas this way, I'll be ready to bet. One of the servants—the chauffeur, or Harvey, or any o' they—they knew, from the stories goin' round after the big accident, that Mrs Milne had that flask in her car, and took a swig on the quiet like—'

'A swig,' said Toby, 'that completely emptied a full flask. People taking swigs on the quiet like, Sam, don't usually do anything to give themselves away so badly.'

'Maybe there was more than one o' them in it. And the last one wouldn't know as the flask was full at the beginnin'.'

Toby chuckled. 'Procession to the drinking well—a sweet picture.'

'Well, Maxwells don't keep no drink of their own in the house, I can tell you that,' said Eggbear. 'And the last one, he'd know the flask was empty, wouldn't he? And then, when it comes out at the inquest as there must be a flask or bottle somewhere around, he sees a chance of makin' trouble—'

'Assuming,' said Toby, 'he's someone with a particular grudge against Mrs Milne. D'you know of anyone?'

'Maybe 'tisn't a particular grudge at all,' said Eggbear,

'but just a grudge against society like, or maybe—' and his face lit up—'he's got a perverted psychology.'

Toby said nothing. He sloped the teacup on his chest, tucked in his chin and drank a little tea. Suddenly he inquired: 'Any inquiries being made in South Africa?'

Eggbear nodded.

'And the steamship company?'

'Yes, there was a third-class passenger called Maxwell on the *Kintyre Castle* last week. Why? Worryin' about that identification, Toby? The old lady's half cracked, that's all there is to that.'

'I want to know more about those Maxwells,' said Toby, 'and about that young man Laws.'

'Just now and then,' muttered the sergeant, 'I find myself wonderin' why you want to know. You're sure you aren't still employed by that newspaper, Toby?'

'Shelley Maxwell,' said Toby ruminatively, ignoring him. 'Shelley Maxwell. That tells you a good deal, doesn't it? His parents meant him to be one of those lucent spirits, shining with the white fire of idealistic—'

'Tobe,' George interrupted, 'if it *was* one of them emptied the flask, it was done before they knew who the dead chap was.'

'Was it?' said Toby. Then: '*Was* it?' Sitting up with a jerk he slopped tea on to his trousers. He looked round him with a glazed kind of stare. 'Please, please,' he rapped out suddenly at Mrs Eggbear, 'tell me all the scandal you know about the Maxwells!'

'You see, George,' said Toby, as the two of them walked back to the inn, 'the major's cottage is only a few minutes walk away from that bit of road, and the house itself isn't so far away. Suppose that Shelley Maxwell wasn't going *to* the house, but coming away from it . . .'

George grunted. 'Suppose,' he said, 'we talked about something else for a while.'

Toby laughed. They were walking through a faint mist, blown in from the sea. It was saltily dank against their faces.

Toby laughed again. Then he started whistling, and, as it happened, they spoke no more until they reached the inn.

The next morning they called together on Mrs Milne.

Ruby was sullen when she admitted them. She shrugged a shoulder at them, strolled across the hall, opened the door of the drawing-room and spoke round it: ' 'Tis those two men from the police, Miss Daphne. Shall I trouble Mrs Milne about'n or not?'

A man's voice answered: 'Oh, splendid! Show them in.' But he did not wait for them to be shown in. As Ruby withdrew a step from the door, pushing it farther open, Adrian Laws came out to meet them.

His copper-coloured hair was ruffled as if affectionate fingers had been wandering through it. He was flattening it with one hand and holding out the other. There were hearty handshakes, explanations that he'd been wishing he could meet them—had heard of Toby Dyke from Eggbear ages ago, felt he was one of those rare people who was really in contact with reality, not someone who, like himself, really did his living at second-hand . . .

'Second-hand?' said Toby incredulously, looking straight past the young man and through the open door at the girl who was lying on the settee, both her head and feet supported by piles of cushions.

She sat up halfway and said: 'Do come in. Have you had another anonymous letter?'

'No,' said Toby, 'but I've been having ideas about the last one.'

'That'll please mother. Sit down. Have a cigarette.' There was not a trace of the shyness she had shown the day before. The stimulated look of her cheeks and of her lips—much redder than the lipstick she used had made them yesterday—suggested she had just been experiencing a fair amount of kissing.

But as soon as her eyes met Toby's she looked at nothing else. 'Over there,' she said, pointing at the enamelled cigarette-box, but without her gaze following her pointing. Neither did she look away from the dark face with its big nose and rather tight-lipped smile as she said: 'Adrian, put those records on the floor. There ought to be room to sit down. You know, Mr Dyke, mother was really awfully angry about that letter. She took it seriously. She said someone was trying to do her down. I think, if you manage to find out who sent it, she'll be tremendously grateful.'

Toby had sat down, as he had been told, had lit a cigarette, and was returning the girl's starry gaze with a brightening in his own which revealed that so far this visit was causing him nothing but pleasure.

'Then she'll see us now?'

'Of *course*,' said Daphne Milne. 'She'll be grateful, I tell you. Anyway, she ought to be. If it was just old Eggbear I know nothing'd happen—though I suppose if it goes on, if there's a poison pen in the village and all that sort of thing, Scotland Yard would get called in, wouldn't they? I know I've read in the papers about Scotland Yard detectives disguising themselves as social workers or American tourists or something, and being put on to watch awfully respectable old women who are sending nasty letters all round to comfort their inhibitions. Only of course it'd be much more thrilling if *you* solved it, Mr Dyke. You're trying to, aren't you?' She spoke very fast, and when she finished her mouth hung open a little as if in an eager breathlessness.

Also enthusiastically, but in a soft, even voice, Adrian Laws said: 'Do tell us what you're doing. Have you tested the letter for fingerprints? Are the letter-boxes being watched? Why d'you want to see Mrs Milne?'

Toby looked round at the young man for a moment. Off-hand in voice and manner, he replied: 'Oh, I just want to ask her about one or two things.'

'As a matter of fact,' said George suddenly—he was sitting in uncomfortable uprightness on the piano-stool—'we want to ask the lady if she'd take us up to see Sir Joseph and Lady Maxwell.'

Daphne frowned in bewilderment, Toby frowned in surprised annoyance, Adrian looked pleased and interested, and Mrs Milne, at that moment, entered.

She appeared extraordinarily tired. It was noticeable at once; her skin sagged, her mouth was pinched, her eyes were dull and peevish. Yet she came in briskly, though there was neither a smile nor any welcome on her face. It might have been some routine interview she was attending.

She ignored both her daughter and Adrian completely. In the glance that the two of them exchanged when they saw this there was understanding and faintly malicious amusement. She apologized to Toby, saying she had been writing letters. Sitting down, she reached with a hurried gesture for a cigarette from the enamelled box.

'Not another letter?' she said, making the same guess as Daphne had made before her.

'No,' said Toby, 'we've come to ask a favour. It's in connection with the letter, though you may not find the connection obvious. I wondered if you could take us to see Sir Joseph and Lady Maxwell.'

She gave them a hard stare. 'In connection with that letter, you say? What an extraordinary idea.' Her short laugh had a contemptuous edge to it. She took quick, nervous puffs at her cigarette.

'I told you,' said Toby, 'the connection isn't obvious—although, of course, it was their son who was killed.'

'Aren't you forgetting,' she said, 'that it was I who killed him?'

'They're refusing to see you?'

Daphne began: 'Mother, they aren't! Mother, you could—'

But Mrs Milne cut across her: 'I haven't given them the opportunity yet. And I think, for the present, that that's the way I'll continue.'

Daphne began again: 'Oh, you *are* mean. Mr Dyke is—'

But this time Adrian made a face at her from across the room and stopped her.

Toby said: 'I wish I could make you change your mind. I'm not asking this in an idle spirit. I've got quite serious reasons.'

'I don't doubt it,' she said, 'but I have my serious reasons for refusing.'

'You realize these letters may continue, may become more annoying and menacing?'

She nodded. 'And it isn't that I want to be obstructive or unappreciative, Mr Dyke, but I know there's no way in which either of the Maxwells could be connected with this business.'

'You know?'

She laughed, flicking ash on to a glass ash tray. 'At least,' she said, 'I know quite a lot about the Maxwells, and I don't believe, Mr Dyke, that you do. In fact, you don't know much about Chovey. Villages are curious places, they take a great deal of penetrating. But if you believe that Sir Joseph or Lady Maxwell would be capable of anything that hadn't a most strictly moral origin—'

'But it's just people like that,' cried Daphne eagerly, 'who do things like writing anonymous letters. It is really. It's their inhibitions. It's their way of revealing all their repressed desires. It's a regression to infantility.'

'I wish,' said her mother in an indifferent voice, 'you wouldn't make a complete fool of yourself, Daphne.'

A jerk of the shoulders, a vivid flush, and Daphne was

on her feet, glaring at her mother with angrily darkened eyes. Then she banged from the room. Mrs Milne continued in the same flat tone: 'That's what she makes of the sort of things you tell her, Adrian.'

The young man smiled. It was the understanding and malicious smile that had flitted across his face a few minutes earlier. He stood up and lounged out after the girl. Mrs Milne stubbed out a half-smoked cigarette and reached for another. She remarked: 'A daughter, Mr Dyke, is an awkward responsibility.'

'To return to the Maxwells . . .' said Toby.

But still she was firm in refusing to take them to Chovey Place, and after a few minutes George and Toby departed.

Out on the drive, walking towards the gate, Toby said: 'Why the hell d'you want to go and blurt out like that what it was we wanted her to do? I was going to say it was an important and private matter, and ask to speak to her alone. I'd have managed her far better without the girl and the not-so-popular lover there. But once you'd given away what it was we wanted, I couldn't very well go on with that.'

George pushed back his cap and scratched the top of his head. 'Matter of fact, I didn't think you'd stand much chance with her anyway, and I thought—' He paused. There were footsteps on the gravel behind them. They both looked round. Adrian Laws was hurrying after them. 'There,' said George, looking modestly at the ground, 'that's what I thought, Tobe.'

Adrian Laws came up to them and started walking between them. 'Look here,' he said, 'I'm awfully sorry she was like that. So's Daphne. She can be damn difficult sometimes. But if you like I'll take you up to the Maxwells. I suppose, actually, it may be a bit awkward for her, though I'm sure Aunt Emmeline wouldn't turn nasty—not really my aunt, by the way; sort of a cousin. But old Joe might be able to find some totally virtuous reason for behaving brutally.'

'Thanks,' said Toby, 'very good of you. Er . . . do we walk there?'

Laws grinned. 'Got my three-wheeler at the gate. Hope you'll be able to pack into it.'

For the first quarter of a mile in the three-wheeler Toby tried to talk. After that he sang. The twelve-year-old, air-cooled engine and rattling mudguards were kinder to his singing than they were to his talk; they drowned no more than was welcome. He sang one of the more cheerful psalms, lifting up his eyes to the brown hills of Dartmoor, five or six miles ahead.

Adrian Laws, coping with direct steering, crouched at the wheel with a tense and furtive concentration, as if he were stalking an enemy. He did not treat his roaring, shaking little car with the proud tenderness that such possessions usually win from their owners; there was a savage if fatalistic dislike in his handling of it, an all too obvious lack of respect for antiquity and cheapness.

'We'll leave it here and walk the rest, if you don't mind,' he said, when they reached the gates of Chovey Place. 'Old Joe won't have it inside the grounds—says the noise scares the wild birds.'

'Pheasants?' asked Toby.

'Oh, dear me, no—no blood-sports hereabouts. Think of every worthy cause you've ever heard of, anti-vivisection, vegetarianism, propagation of the knowledge of the Higher Life—one or other of my dear relatives sends in a regular subscription. Not both of them, not by any means—that's where the fun comes in. There's lots of quiet fun in that household, unlikely as that may seem to you, taking a casual look at the place.'

The casual look they were taking through the tall, wrought-iron gates showed them gloomy, Victorian battlements about half a mile away.

'Is that where you live yourself?' said Toby.

'Good Lord, no! I've a cottage on the edge of the moor—well, you can call it a cottage if you've a civil disposition. It's a converted cowhouse, rapidly reverting to its original beliefs.'

'Lived there long?'

'Since last spring. Thought—' his voice put ironic quotation marks round the words—'my spirit needed the refreshment of solitude. Damn fool idea. Don't know why I've stayed so long.'

Toby looked amused. He remarked: 'Not much love lost between that mother and daughter, is there?'

Adrian shrugged. 'I'd put it the other way round, myself. Too much love lost—possessive, domineering love.' He pushed open the gate, and the three of them passed through. 'You've no idea the trouble I'm having, getting Daphne to fight that woman's influence.'

Toby was setting a pretty slow pace towards those grey, stucco battlements.

'Got a good deal of money, hasn't she?' he said.

'Mrs Milne? Should think she must have.'

'Where's it come from?'

Adrian gave a sudden, sharp laugh. Toby echoed it. 'Yes,' he said, 'I know I'm pumping you. Got to pump somebody.'

'Yes,' said Adrian thoughtfully. There was still amusement on his face, but it looked like a calculating amusement, secret, derisive. 'Yes, if you like,' he said, his voice taking on its softer, smoother tone, 'but hasn't anyone mentioned to you yet that when it comes to matters of fact I'm not noticeably reliable?'

'No one's bothered to mention anything much about you up to the present.'

Adrian put on a look of exaggerated disappointment. 'What a thing to say to the local celebrity. Why, my name's familiar to the homes of England—at least five hundred of them. My novel sold five hundred copies. You, I take it—' he gave Toby a sidelong glance—'haven't got a home?'

'Quite right,' said Toby. 'Now about Mrs Milne. Her money comes from . . .?'

Adrian made a resigned gesture. 'Her money comes from the same place as mine ought to—Paternoster Row. We draw it from different numbers and in different quantities, and, I like to think, for different reasons, but—'

Toby interrupted: 'You mean she writes?'

'Writes, gets money: speculates, gets more money. That's the story. Or, if you like it in fewer words still—luck! Unholy, undeserved luck.' This time there was a cut in Adrian's soft laugh. 'Heard of Wendy Bartlemy?'

Toby whistled. 'Is *that* who she is? I don't mean I've read any of them, but one sees them everywhere. Sex boiled in treacle, that's the formula, isn't it?'

'And dished up lukewarm on a plate of Devon pottery. She's damn clever, really. It's a deliberate game, tongue well in cheek, and she hits it off perfectly.'

Toby frowned, strolling on at the same slow pace.

'I sort of remember—wasn't there a stunt some years back?—seem to remember being mixed up in it myself. A newspaper outcry suddenly about Who *Is* Wendy Bartlemy? It was the usual publicity racket, but, for once, nothing came out. She'd got herself remarkably well hidden.'

'Reckon you can't have been *really* interested in the case, Tobe,' said George.

Toby admitted that that was probable. Adrian said indifferently: 'I don't remember anything about that. I confess that normally I'm not much interested in the Wendy Bartlemys. But when I discovered I knew her—it was Daphne who told me—I was rather intrigued. Fitting the books and the woman together, you know. In the process I've come to—admire her, shall I call it, enormously.'

'Oh, yes?' said Toby.

'Yes, really,' said Adrian blandly.

'She doesn't reciprocate, does she?'

'Well, d'you know—I dare say you won't believe it—she's extraordinarily jealous of me.'

'Oh, yes?' said Toby again.

Adrian smiled at him. 'I know it sounds ridiculous, she with her God-knows-how-many editions, and me with my measly five hundred copies. But she knows I've got something she hasn't.'

'Artistic integrity?'

Adrian took it without self-consciousness. 'Yes. As a matter of fact, you often come across the same thing in these business people—an amazing sense of inferiority when they meet a man whose soul is still his own.'

'Grand for the soul-capitalist,' said Toby.

Adrian went on: 'Of course, it's really that that's at the bottom of the trouble. She's fiendishly jealous of me, and that makes her furious that I of all people should be getting influence over Daphne. Poor girl, it's time somebody did. All the same, I do admire—'

'I do admire, yes, I do admire my girl's mother—she's more than a mother to me!' The end of the sentence turned into song.

Adrian, tight-lipped, turned a furious face on Toby. But in a moment the anger had slid off it. There was a good-natured, ironic light in the eyes behind the spectacles. The three of them walked on for a while in silence.

They were almost at the house when Toby suddenly asked: 'D'you know why she does it?'

'Does what?'

'Hides up the Wendy Bartlemy business. There's never even been a photograph in the papers.'

Eyes still good-natured and ironic met Toby's, but the

voice had an insulting bite in it. 'I'm not sure,' said Adrian, 'that if I knew I'd tell you.'

Toby shrugged. They went on up to the house.

A vast, cold hall, an acreage of polished floorboards, a wide, carpetless, highly polished stair, a number of tall, mahogany doors, an oak chest with the date 1631 carved on it, a bad painting of a stream, a few rocks and some heather—that was all there was to see when Adrian pushed open the door. There was a radiator to one side, but it made the place no warmer than it would have been had someone lit a gas-ring for a few minutes to boil a kettle. The place had the unfriendliness of one of the older tube stations.

Adrian said: 'You'd better wait here while I go on and talk to Aunt Emmeline. I'll make the story fit the way she takes the idea of seeing you—you won't mind, will you?' And he left them, disappearing through one of the mahogany doors.

Toby strolled towards the picture and stood in front of it.

'George—' he was speaking only just above a whisper—'what d'you think of that young man? Cares a hell of a lot about having no money, doesn't he?'

'Eh? Well, who doesn't?'

'Oh, quite. Vain too, wouldn't you say?'

George said nothing, but a movement of his ear signalled a caution to Toby. A door behind them opened, and Adrian came quickly across the hall.

'Hullo, admiring Uncle Joe's handiwork? This house is full of his execrable paintings of Dartmoor. No other pictures in it except a few photographs of the Acropolis, taken with Uncle Joe's own little camera and enlarged in the village. Well, she'll see you; in fact, she's wild to see you. I've told her that you're a reporter and that you've got hold of the story of her saying that it wasn't Bish who was killed. There was a reporter here from the local paper yesterday, and old Joe turned him out without letting her know; she's mad about it. She hopes you're from one of the *very* big nationals. Come along.' Adrian led them into the drawing-room.

There was a fire there, and the room was not really cold, but because of its size and its austerity, the uprightness of its chairs, the harsh blue of the linen curtains and its extreme cleanliness, there was the same chill in its atmosphere as in that of the hall. The little woman who sat on the settee close to the fire had a fur wrap round her shoulders.

She rose and came with her small, doddering steps to greet them.

'I feel I've met you before, haven't I?' she said, keeping hold of Toby's hand and peering up into his face. Her blue eyes looked as if they were struggling, through a lifetime's absent-mindedness, to concentrate. 'Well, it doesn't matter, does it? I'm so grateful to you for coming, and to Adrian for thinking of bringing you. He has such—' she smiled with a sort of roguishness, as if she were about to bring out a very daring slang expression—'such "bright" ideas sometimes. I've been so bewildered—yes, and very much hurt—by the extraordinary things that have been happening. Hurt by the pigheadedness of people, you know. Now come and sit down and let's discuss the whole matter.'

Pattering back to her seat, she indicated chairs for Toby and George. But when Adrian sat down on the arm of her settee she gave him a look which showed that she had not expected him to remain. Adrian, however, disregarded it.

'Now where shall we begin?' she asked Toby eagerly.

There was a perplexed look on his face. He took a moment to answer. Then he gave an amused smile.

'One place is as good as another, I should say. I'd rather like to go right to the beginning, but you'd prefer the middle, I imagine. Well then, why is it you don't think that the man who was killed is your son?'

She gave a reproving shake of her head. 'It really isn't a question of think, Mr Dyke. I *know*.'

'All right, then: on what do you base your knowledge?'

'Not,' she replied immediately, 'on what you're expecting. I know you're expecting me to say on woman's intuition. That's the way my husband's been trying to put me off; he says I've been trying to oppose a mere intuition to his unprejudiced judgment. As if I should dream of doing such a thing! Why, Mr Dyke, d'you know that my Christian name is the same as Mrs Pankhurst's and Mrs Pethick Lawrence's? I don't mean,' she added hurriedly, 'that I want to put myself on a level with them; my part in the great struggle was a *very* small one; with my health it couldn't have been otherwise. But what I mean to say is that I consider myself quite as able to look at the facts that are staring at me as any man, or at any rate—' the shrewdness that sometimes lit her face glinted there for a moment now—'as my husband.'

'Good,' said Toby. 'Now, if I remember rightly, when you went to view the body, as they say, you touched one of the hands . . .'

Her face was startled, her wrinkled cheeks were suddenly flushed with red. 'Why, how very, very—' But she broke off and said: 'Of course, that's where I saw you—and your friend, Mr—er . . .?'

'Porphyrus,' muttered George.

'Yes, I remember you both quite clearly now.'

'The hand . . .' Toby repeated.

But she would not take the lead. She settled the fur wrap closer about her shoulders, and in doing so remarked: 'I expect you think it's odd of me wearing a wrap like this in the house, but I find it so hard to keep warm. And this fur is really very cosy—though it's very old. It belonged to a dear aunt of mine. My husband disapproves of my wearing fur, but I find that sentimental. I have the deepest aversion to blood-sports, and of course I'm a vegetarian, but there my reasons are purely dietetic. Now where was I? . . . Ah yes, I was going to give you some facts. First, then: that poor man was dead drunk, also he was almost without money. My son would not have been in either condition.'

'I see,' said Toby. He looked at the floor, at the shining boards that sent up a faint odour of wax polish. 'How many years is it, Lady Maxwell, since you saw your son?'

With a trace of defiance in her voice she answered: 'About ten.'

'And you're sure that after ten years . . .?'

'I've told you I'm going entirely on facts, Mr Dyke. I've been hearing from—from a friend, at quite frequent intervals, a friend who knows Shelley. He assures me that during the last few years Shelley's altered into an—an altogether more serious person. You know, that was all that was the matter when he was younger; he wasn't serious. Of course, seriousness is very important; flippancy, insincerity, they're detestable qualities, aren't they? But perhaps when one's young . . .' She looked with a kind of appeal at Toby. There was a deep sadness in her voice and she left the sentence inconclusive.

Adrian leant over her and put an arm round her shoulders. There was a teasing smile on his face. 'You know, Aunt Emmeline, you're talking as if Dyke knew the shadier side of our family history.'

'Adrian!'

His teasing smile broadened. 'After all, we've kept it so carefully from the village gossips, haven't we?' He looked up at Toby. 'Or haven't we?' he asked softly.

'Yes and no,' said Toby.

Her blue eyes were puzzled, her sunken lips worked together nervously. 'I don't understand. Why need we go into all that?'

'I'm afraid I don't know,' said Toby. 'It's Mr Laws who seems to like the idea.'

'Me?' said Adrian. 'Oh no. Oh no, no, no.'

She looked at him suspiciously. His face was bland. She turned again to Toby. '*Do* the village people know about it, Mr Dyke? Have they been telling you things?'

'I haven't talked to many of the village people,' he replied, 'except Eggbear, who's an old friend of mine, and his wife. From their slightly curious insistence on how little they knew about it I rather jumped to the conclusion that it was something it would have been a bit inconvenient for them to know. After all—they *are* the police.'

She sighed. 'Adrian,' she said suddenly, 'I think some tea would be very pleasant. Would you please go and tell Harvey that we'd like some tea? I often like tea in the middle of the morning, don't you, Mr Dyke? You don't mind going, do you, Adrian dear? I never ring for Harvey if I can help it; he's so very busy.'

Adrian slid off the arm of the settee. 'All right, Aunt Emmeline, and I won't be too quick about it.' He lounged out of the room.

She made a fluttering gesture with her small hands. 'I'm afraid I'm not very good at young people, Mr Dyke. They fluster me. I—' She was distraught for a moment, staring at the door that Adrian had closed behind him. She was fingering the chain round her neck, the same chain of carnelian, amber, topaz and agate that Toby had noticed before. Realizing that she was fingering it, she suddenly took it off and held it out to Toby, asking him if he didn't think it an interesting necklace. 'The topaz came from Cornwall; an uncle of mine—he was a clergyman—collected them for me. And the amber came from the east coast, where my sister used to live. She was married to a clergyman. There are an *extraordinary* number of clergymen in my family.' She gave an unexpected little titter.

As Toby handed back the chain she began again: 'Now I've made up my mind I'm going to tell you all about that wretched old business. I know I can trust you not to repeat it. Yes, somehow I know I can trust you. And after all, from me you'll hear the correct story, not the dreadful misrepresentation you might be given by other people. Well, our son Shelley was a very wild boy, always. High-spirited, hot-headed. He enjoyed life tremendously. But he never got on at all well with his father. I don't really think it was the fault of either of them. It was just that they were two such very different people, you see. I dare say there've been cases in your own experience just like that?'

Toby admitted that there had.

She went on: 'As Shelley grew older—perhaps I should say, as my husband grew older too—the quarrels became more serious. Sometimes they were *very* disquieting. I used to worry a great deal. Shelley was always running into debt. There were—other things too, I think, but it was only his debts he brought home to us. He was really very good at managing his own difficulties, very self-reliant and independent. But when he couldn't pay his debts and there were people clamouring at him, well, he had to come to us, hadn't he?' She paused for Toby to nod agreement. 'Well, my husband paid his creditors two or three times. He wouldn't have liked other people to suffer, you see, for his son's recklessness, but the last time he gave Shelley some very solemn warnings. Yet it happened again. That time my husband said no, and was quite, quite firm; neither of us could have any effect on him. Shelley went away in a dreadful rage, saying he'd never come near us again—of course, he didn't mean it. And then . . . then, you see, Mr Dyke, Shelley wrote his father's name on a cheque, and—wrote it rather badly. The person he asked to cash the cheque took it without saying anything, cashed it for him, then sent it to my husband. My husband, of course, sent him the money he had, so to speak, loaned our son, but he told Shelley that unless he went abroad he would put the cheque in the hands of the police. Oh, of course he wouldn't have really done it, Mr Dyke—my husband isn't as hard as that, indeed he isn't hard at all, only limited in some directions. But that's ten years ago, and . . .' She sighed again, very deeply.

After a moment Toby prompted: 'And he went to South Africa?'

She nodded. There was a tense, flushed look on her delicately shaped features, as if telling the story had produced an excitement within her that she had no means to express.

'But you hear from him?'

'From friends,' she said quickly, 'who've told me how well he's got on, how well he's turned out. After all, he was quite young when it happened—not much over thirty.'

'But you write to him, don't you?' asked Toby gently.

'My friends . . .' she began, but then she stopped. She peered into Toby's face with a dazed yet urgent questioning. 'If I tell you, you won't—you won't—?'

'No,' said Toby, 'I won't tell your husband.'

She got up and doddered across to a bureau in the corner of the room. Crouching in front of it, she pulled out the bottom drawer. From it she took a bundle of letters.

As she was pushing the drawer in again Toby said: 'You don't lock it?'

Her glance was cold and astonished. 'My husband would *never* look amongst my private papers. Now—' she came back to her seat by the fire—'here are all the letters that Shelley's written to me during these ten years. Not very many; he isn't what I was brought up to think a good correspondent. But they're such interesting letters. He gets so much into them in quite a few lines; that's the real art of writing, isn't it? Now you take a look at them and tell me—could the man who wrote them have arrived here drunk and penniless?'

Toby took the bundle and untied the coloured tape that held it together. He began to read the letters. After the first two or three he began to skip, glancing at the beginning, which was generally thanks for money his mother had sent him, and at the end, which was generally a request for more. They contained frequent assurances of his steadily improving character, now and then there were highly adjectival descriptions of scenery, occasionally there was a quite amusingly told anecdote. But in their way they were certainly skilful letters, letters his mother would probably find brilliant, affectionate and satisfying. For instance, there were many reminders of whimsical little jokes they had had between them, jokes that would have lingered with an ever-increasing sweetness in the memory of a very lonely woman.

Suddenly Toby looked up. 'This one's in a different writing.'

She was watching every movement of his face as he sat reading. She nodded brightly. 'It's written with his left hand.'

He was reading the letter. 'Ah, I see, he'd cut himself.'

'Poor boy,' she said, 'he must have had a dreadful time with it. A poisoned arm in a sling for weeks—I sent him rather more money than usual because of it, because I didn't want to have him trying to get on without a doctor or anything like that.'

'And that was why you looked at his—the man's hand?'

She nodded again with a vivid smile. 'And there was no scar,' she said triumphantly, 'not a trace of one!'

Toby went on reading. The next letter was still in the wobbly, left-hand writing, but after that the normal writing resumed. Shelley Maxwell worked, it appeared, in a canning firm. He never said much about what he did there, but reiterated that he was on excellent social terms with his employers.

The last letter but one in the bundle was in the wobbly, unskilled writing.

'Hullo, he's cut himself again,' said Toby.

'No,' she said, 'he broke his wrist.'

'Poor boy,' murmured Toby.

'Did he get more money for that too?' asked George.

She turned to him startled, as if, until he spoke, she had forgotten his presence. 'Why yes,' she said. 'I was very anxious about him.'

Toby nodded. The careful expressionlessness of his face gave it grimness. He held the bundle of letters out to Lady Maxwell.

Before she could take it, George took it from him. He retied the tape round it, making a neat bow, then handed it on to her. She started toward the bureau with the bundle held tenderly in her two hands.

'And now you must tell me,' she said, 'how you mean to set about—' But the sentence was broken off and she made a dive for the bureau like a rabbit scurrying to its hole at the sound of a gun.

On the path outside the french window, looking in at them, stood Major Maxwell.

CHAPTER 8

She closed the drawer of the bureau, stood up shakily and undid the catch of the window.

Easy in his movements like a young man, Major Maxwell stepped inside. The gaze from his singularly bright brown eyes went straight past his sister-in-law to

Toby and George, standing on the hearth-rug.

In her nervousness Lady Maxwell's slow and over-articulated speech became even slower, even more precious in its enunciation. Her introductions took an amazingly long time. Only after several false starts, repetitions and embarrassing little jokes, she at length came round to saying: 'Mr Dyke and Mr Pollinger are friends of Adrian's, Stuart.'

In a lazy, sceptical voice he answered: 'Really?'

Her sunken lips were working together. 'I ordered tea . . . It ought to be here . . . Oh, and did you sleep any better last night, Stuart? If you didn't I really think you ought to see someone. But don't let him make you take drugs, whatever you do. You won't, will you? They do you no good, you know, they don't *cure* the trouble. But I can let you have some stuff that sensible herbal man in Bognor gave me. It isn't a drug at all, it just has a gentle, soothing—'

'I'm perfectly well, thanks, Emmie,' said the major. He said it, however, with an emphasis that suggested he was conscious of smudges under his eyes and the sagging look of his face, where usually the skin seemed to be drawn so cleanly over the bones. He went on quickly: 'Don't mind my coming in in gum-boots, do you? The ground's as hard as iron; I haven't picked up any mud. Find our neighbourhood interesting, Mr Dyke?' The slurred, lazy voice was curiously at variance with the wearily expressive face.

His eyes holding the other man's in an interchange which on both sides was faintly hostile and faintly amused, Toby answered: 'Unexpectedly.'

'Good,' said Stuart Maxwell.

He turned back to his sister-in-law who had returned to her corner of the settee and was folding her fur wrap around her.

'I just came in to tell you, Emmie, that I'd met Miss

Willis. She said she was sure you weren't expecting her and her father to lunch today, and that when you wrote to her you must have made a mistake. But she asked me just to clear the matter up for her. I said of course there was a mistake of some kind.'

'A mistake?' said Lady Maxwell. There was gentle wonder in her tone. 'Today's Saturday, isn't it? I wrote on Thursday evening and asked them to lunch on Saturday. I can't think of any mistake I can have made in that.'

His breath came in a sigh between clenched teeth. 'My dear Emmie, don't put it on. Whatever attitude you've decided to take up, don't pretend you've forgotten we've got a funeral this afternoon.'

She looked away from him with a little smile, which, as her eyes met Toby's, became conspiratorial. 'Oh, I'm so glad you're going to the funeral of that poor, unknown man, Stuart. Whoever he is, why should he go to his grave as if no one anywhere had ever cared for him? Indeed I'm glad you're going, my dear. There's something so sordid, so indescribably mean about a lonely burial.'

'For God's sake—' he began.

'But I'm afraid I can't go myself,' she ran on. 'It's the standing about in the cold, you know; it'd be foolish of me to risk it, and not really considerate, because getting ill only means trouble for other people. Oh, Stuart—' her voice went suddenly reproachful—'not in here . . .' For the major had taken a pipe out of his pocket and was starting to fill it.

He went on filling it with fierce, prodding fingers. 'D'you mean to say,' he said, 'that you came home after the inquest on Thursday and sat straight down and wrote asking the Willises to lunch today—the day that had just been arranged for the funeral? You did that deliberately?'

Her eyes were on his pipe. His disregard of her remonstrance seemed to have filled her with trembling anger. 'Naturally I didn't do it in my sleep,' she said. 'I have never, to my knowledge, sent anyone an invitation which I had not written deliberately, consciously, or, as you might put it, when I was in full possession of my faculties.'

'Such as they are,' he muttered under his breath. He struck a match. 'The Willises,' he said aloud, sucking at his pipe, 'had better go on thinking it was a mistake.'

She raised a small, brown hand and hammered with it on the arm of the settee. 'I can think of no reason,' she said, 'I can think of no reason at all, why you should have interfered with the arrangements for my little luncheon party.'

Another exasperated sigh drove sudden wreaths of smoke in front of his face. He threw the used match at the fireplace. 'They wouldn't like it, you know. They wouldn't like being used as a scoreboard in a family quarrel. It'd make them feel foolish. I imagine they'd be inclined not to forgive you.'

On the hearth-rug George shifted from foot to foot in embarrassment, Toby stood squarely, looking on.

Lady Maxwell said: 'I'm hoping to discover that the neighbourhood isn't as much under Joseph's thumb as you seem to think it is. And truly, I don't understand why you should take for granted that his word should be accepted rather than mine. No, Stuart, I don't understand that. You're usually so fair-minded. I'm afraid I feel disappointed.'

'The coroner accepted Joe's word, Emmie. Besides—' he was trying to control his impatience, to make his voice sound quiet and reasonable—'what motive could Joe have in saying his son was dead if he wasn't? Mr Dyke, can you suggest a motive? Don't mind how discreditable it sounds, but make it rational. Why should a father pretend a corpse was his son if it wasn't? Now if it were the son who was doing the pretending—'

'Stuart!' She had started to her feet. The anger on her

face was immediately succeeded by a look of intense pain. The major looked away from her.

'Sorry, Emmie,' he said. 'Dyke, are you doing anything special at the moment? Come down to the cottage and have a drink.'

The sitting-room in the major's cottage was a small room, comfortably and pleasantly furnished, though perhaps with a slightly too conscious masculinity; pipe-racks and tobacco-jars caught the eye, the chairs were very leathery. But the whisky was all right, and the fire of split logs gave out satisfying warmth.

The major's Aberdeen got to its feet in the armchair where it had been sleeping, to bark at the visitors. Turned out of the chair, it nosed about the room for a while, then jumped on to its master's knees and went to sleep again. Stuart Maxwell ruffled the hair behind its ears with a sensitively caressing hand. Toby looked at the two, the man and the dog.

'Trustful animals, dogs,' he remarked. He was sunk low in the deep chair, his eyes were narrowed to sleepy slits. 'And if you come to think of it, so are humans.'

'Well, you can't get very far without trusting people to some extent,' said Maxwell, 'can you?'

'Can't you?' said Toby.

Maxwell gave a quiet laugh. 'Personally, I don't find suspicion worth while. Exhausting business.'

'Quite,' said Toby. 'Keeps one awake at night.'

Again the major laughed. He was looking down at the dog on his knees. 'I've an indolent nature,' he said. 'Simple trust is doubtless the laziest way of dealing with the uncertain. With you, I suppose, suspicion's a professional asset. I'd be no good at your job.'

'My job?' said Toby.

'This left hand of the police business.'

'Well, never mind about that. Go ahead and ask me

what you're wanting to.' A sudden grin lit up his face.

Stuart Maxwell gazed at him for a moment. Then he reached for the decanter and refilled his own glass. He drank it quickly. 'You've a certain reputation hereabouts, you know,' he said. 'That's Eggbear's fault. But the result of it is, unbelievable as it may seem to you, that one might be interested in making your acquaintance—for its own sake, so to speak.'

'So you brought me here without wanting to ask me anything in particular?'

Maxwell nodded.

'All right,' said Toby, 'go ahead and ask.'

Pushing the dog off his knees, the major stood up. Suddenly his face was the same face that had glared at Sergeant Eggbear in the bar of the Ring of Bells, a face that was tense with a cold and vicious anger. But today there was tiredness and nervousness there as well. It was a ravaged face, as if there were a strain upon the man that was almost past bearing.

'There's nothing I want to ask you, but here's something I'm going to tell you. Keep your damned interfering nose out of the affairs of my family!'

'I'm not at all sure,' said Toby slowly, 'that they *are* the affairs of your family.'

Maxwell sneered. But already there was something more relaxed about his posture, the moment of uncontrolled fury was past. He turned away, looking down at the fire.

George's hand shot out for the decanter. He filled Maxwell's glass, setting the decanter noiselessly down again. Maxwell stirred one of the logs with the toe of his slipper.

'You don't mean to tell me,' he said, 'that you're giving any credence to my sister-in-law's delusions?'

'Why not?' said Toby. 'Is she given to delusions?'

Maxwell laughed. He sat down again, his hand going out for his glass. 'She isn't certifiable. As a matter of fact, she's nothing but a rather silly, lonely old woman. Very lonely.'

'Look here,' said Toby, suddenly sitting forward in his chair, 'will you explain to me why it is that everyone takes for granted that your brother's word is better than his wife's?'

'Very lonely,' the major repeated. 'Poor Emmie. Poor old Emmie. Lovely girl once, now just a lonely old woman. I'm very sorry for her. And I'm sorry I spoke to you like I did, Dyke. Hope you'll forgive me. Lonely myself, that's the trouble. You lose your sense of balance when you're lonely, you know. Have another drink.' He filled his own glass again.

Toby slid back into the depths of the chair. The dog jumped up on to Maxwell's knees again. Maxwell stroked the rough fur and sighed. 'I've got Staggers here,' he said, 'no one but Staggers.'

'D'you know,' said Toby, 'I shouldn't mind seeing that brother of yours sometime?'

A broad smile suddenly replaced the melancholy on the major's face. It was pretty flushed by now; the eyes had an oily look. 'You wouldn't like him,' he said. 'Not your type at all. Don't like him myself. Can't stand him. Hate him. Ha, ha, don't believe I've ever told anyone that before. Hate him, ha, ha! That's good, isn't it? Now I'll tell you something, Dyke. D'you know why I went into the army? So's to be different from Joe. Absolutely my only reason for it, ab-ss-solutely.'

'And yet,' said Toby, 'you believe him rather than his wife.'

'Well, I mean to say, Dyke, look at the circumstances. That's it, look at the circumstances. Look at the circumstances. That's all you have to do. Poor lonely old woman, can't believe her son's dead. Can't believe it myself, but that's different. Young Shelley dead! "Oh, weep for Adonais, he is dead—" No, that was Keats, wasn't it? I'm a little mixed up this morning. Tired. Haven't been sleeping. Things go round and round in here.' He bored with his finger at his temple, and drank.

'Yes,' said Toby, 'round and round. Suspicions, for instance.'

'All sorts of things,' said the major. 'There was a Boche in the war. Stone dead. Magnificent fellow, long as this room. Stretched out flat, stone dead. My batman started going through his pockets. "You can't do that," I said, "it's robbing the dead." Fellow went on doing it. Hadn't time to stop him. That goes round in here.' Again he made that boring motion with his finger against his temple. It was an agonized gesture. 'Magnificent,' he muttered, 'long as this room—robbing the dead. Joe's fault I went into the army. Joe's fault I didn't marry Iris. Joe's fault if I don't—' Suddenly he pulled himself up and sat staring at Toby with a look of distraction.

'Yes?' said Toby.

'I'm a little drunk, Dyke. Sorry. Hope it doesn't annoy you. Haven't been sleeping, you see—makes one lose hold of oneself. I wouldn't be talking to you like this if I weren't drunk. But I like you, you're a good chap. I'll tell you about Iris—'

'And about Anna too,' Toby suggested.

'No, no, Iris,' said the major with swift irritation. 'Don't want to talk about Anna to anyone. Mustn't talk, you know, wouldn't be right. But Iris is long ago. She was the most beautiful girl. Lovely eyes. Beautiful. She was Irish and Italian, mixed—*mélange, en français*—beautiful. Joe's fault . . .' His chin had sunk forward on his chest, his hand lay inert and heavy on the dog's head. 'But you can believe him, you know, Dyke. Joe'd never tell a lie. Too holy for that, damn him, damn him, damn him . . .'

'Well, George,' said Toby, out in the sharp, midday air once more, 'it looked like a good idea making him drunk, but what d'you think you got out of it?'

George shook his head dubiously. 'It just came to me as the natural thing, Tobe.'

'There was something I wanted to get out of him sober,' said Toby. 'I wanted to find out *why* everyone believes this Holy Joe.'

'Don't you?' said George.

They were walking down the path towards the stile that would take them on to the Purbrook road close to where the accident had happened.

'I don't know if I do or I don't,' said Toby. 'Strikes me he's just as liable to make a mistake as the old woman is—meaning an honest mistake—and just as liable to be wrong by mistake on purpose, if you get me. If she's in a state of not being able to believe her son's dead, I shouldn't wonder if he's been wanting that son dead for a long time, and got himself into a state where he could easily fancy himself into certainty about any conveniently unrecognizable corpse. No, George, I'm not going to swallow Joe's word just because it's Joe's word. He could have a nice, psychological motive for his belief just as well as his wife could for hers. And then, leaving out the sentiment, mothers generally do know something about their sons' bodies.'

'Don't that soldier-man hate the old boy?' said George. 'Anyway, you'd never have found that out with him sober.'

Toby nodded thoughtfully. 'And he's a peculiar man, is Major Maxwell. There's his temper, the cold, ugly sort of temper of a man who's never given in to his emotions, but hasn't managed to annihilate them either. Then there's his insomnia—recent, I gathered from what his sister-in-law said to him. What keeps a man awake o' nights, George?'

'Women,' said George, 'or lack of same.'

'Or indigestion, of lack of exercise, or an uneasy

conscience. You know, I could go on talking quite a long time about that major. He's intelligent, he's imaginative, he's emotional, he's—'

'He tells lies,' said George.

They had reached the end of the field path, and George had already climbed the stile and was standing on the road.

Toby, one leg swung over the stile, paused. 'What?'

'You come here and look,' said George.

Toby came to his side and stood looking along the road towards Purbrook. It ran level and straight to the point where the main road to Plymouth crossed it, but almost immediately beyond the crossing it rose over another of the humpbacked bridges so common hereabouts. A fairly steady stream of cars was passing along the main road.

'I don't get it,' said Toby.

'Remember when Eggbear was telling us the whole business?' said George. 'Well, he told us how he sent one of his coppers out to ask Maxwell if he'd noticed anyone around when Mrs Milne dropped him at this stile, and—'

'Hey,' Toby broke in, his eyes eager, 'she didn't drop him at any stile. She dropped him up there at the cross-roads. Obviously. She was going on to drop a Miss Someone-or-other somewhere down the main road. Well, she wouldn't have driven down this little bit and then driven back; she'd have stopped at the corner and Maxwell would have got out and walked to the stile. Only . . .' He stopped and looked at George with sudden wariness. 'Is this news to you, George, or have you got it all worked out for yourself?'

'More or less news to me,' George reassured him. 'Go on, tell me.'

Toby looked relieved. He pointed down at their feet. 'Well, d'you see that drip of oil?'

'Oh, that. I'd seen that,' said George. 'If it was Mrs Milne's car—and, matter of fact, it'd got a pretty good drip, I noticed that in the garage—well, if it was her car, of course it means she stopped here on her way back after she'd dropped the other woman, and probably had a chat with Maxwell, who hadn't gone straight home, like he said, but had been waiting for her. That's *if* it was her car. But it's several days ago, Tobe, and all sorts of people stop their cars near stiles, don't they, especially if the stiles have got good hedges each side.'

'All right,' grunted Toby disgustedly, 'forget about it. Go on about the major's lies.'

'Well,' said George, 'when Maxwell was questioned about whether he'd seen anyone coming down the road from Purbrook after he'd been dropped here, he didn't just say no he didn't think so, like you or I would've done. He said no he knew he hadn't seen anyone. And how did he know? He said he'd looked down the road and seen a car's headlights a good way off, so that if anyone had been coming along he'd have been sure to see him against them. But if the car was a good way off he couldn't have seen anyone against the headlights until the person had come over that bridge. Don't know how you feel about it, Tobe, but I'm inclined to think myself that there's a sort of phoney smell about that little bit of evidence.'

Toby nodded. 'And even if cars do stop for other purposes, I'm inclined to think that drip of oil . . . But we've a hell of a walk back to Chovey. We ought to have gone back by the house and picked up Laws and his three-wheeler.'

They started their walk. After about a quarter of an hour Toby said that when they got back to the inn he was going to ask Tom Warren where they could hire a car for the next few days. He said little else. The look of concentration on his face made it savage. George did not try to keep up.

However, when he saw Toby walk straight past the Ring of Bells and make for the police station, he sprinted for thirty yards or so and asked him what he thought he was at.

'I want one more look at Shelley Maxwell before they put him away for good,' said Toby. 'I want to verify whether or not there was a cut on his hand.'

'Going to tell Eggbear about this morning?'

'Not at the moment,' said Toby.

But neither did he tell George, ten minutes later, what he made of the fact that the dead man who lay in the shed behind the police station had indeed no scar on his right hand. He hurried on to his lunch in the same frowning absent-mindedness. George had to draw his attention to the two letters addressed to him that were stuck behind the tapes of the letter-board.

As he looked, Toby came out of his brooding with a shout. He tore the first envelope open. Letters cut out of a newspaper and pasted on to a sheet of cheap, thin paper spelled the message: 'BONFIRES ARE FOR BURNING THINGS AREN'T THEY? WELL WHAT ABOUT A PAIR OF TROUSERS?'

CHAPTER 9

The second letter Toby scarcely glanced at. It had not come by post, but must have been delivered by hand during the morning. It ran:

'Dear Mr Dyke,

'I realize I was abrupt and unfriendly this morning. I am sorry. I have a number of things on my mind and am a good deal worried. You will understand, too that at the moment I am not at all sure of my relations with the Maxwells, and prefer to wait until they have shown their attitude towards me. I wish, however, that I had been less ungracious. I do not want to seem ungrateful for your attempts to discover the source of this annoying letter. I hope you will forgive me.

'Yours sincerely,

'Anna Milne.'

'We'll think about that later,' said Toby, putting it on one side. 'And personally I'm not thinking much about the other either till I've got some food into me. Country air and walking's good for the appetite, isn't it, George?'

'Maybe,' said George, 'but this is an unhealthy neighbourhood.'

'I wouldn't argue the point,' said Toby in a tone of satisfaction.

George made a sound of disgust, and Toby, staring at the anonymous letter which he had propped up against the flower-vase on the table, grinned with a kind of wolfishness.

About an hour later, in the warm and quiet coffee-room, Toby suddenly sat up on the couch by the fire on which he had been stretched in apparent sleep, and said: 'Come on, George, we're seeing about that car. I'm getting tired of being taken to places and dropped there. I want some horse-power, or I'll never get anywhere in this business.'

'Why,' said George, 'where've you got to go to now?'

'Paying some more calls. And if you run into Eggbear, don't mention it. I want to work this my own way. Come on.' And he strode through to the office. There, at an untidy desk, Tom Warren was dozing.

'Where can I hire a car?' said Toby.

Tom Warren rubbed heavy eyes and lit a cigarette.

'Bowdens have a car they hire out sometimes—Bowdens' Garage, just past the school. 'Tis a 1921 Sunbeam. That do you? There was a commercial gent who—'

'Thanks,' said Toby, and left.

'Here, Tobe,' said George, trotting after him, 'where you going to? For the Lord's sake, why can't you settle down a bit?'

'Bowdens' Garage,' said Toby, 'just past the school. That'll be over there. Come on. I only like walking for pleasure, for business I want wheels.'

He crossed the village street, and, by ignoring most of what the Bowden who attended to him said about the weather, the accident, his garden and a burst pipe, succeeded in securing the use of a spacious and venerable Sunbeam in little over a quarter of an hour.

'All right, all right,' said George, taking his seat beside Toby in the car, 'it don't matter that there was a perfectly good Edgar Wallace in the hotel, don't matter about antagonizing the locals by obstructing their natural desires for friendly conversation, it don't matter that I personally am in need of a rest. But where are we going?'

'Back to The Laurels.'

'And after that?'

'Just try a little guessing,' said Toby.

When they were about halfway to the house they passsed a girl walking towards the village. She was walking almost in the middle of the road, her head bent, her hands deep in the pockets of her loose, tweed coat. Absently, without looking up, she got out of the way of their car. Her head was bare and her hair was brightly fair in the sloping afternoon sunlight. Her walk was slow and listless.

'So it isn't her you're going to see,' said George, as Toby did not even slow down.

'No, it's the mother again.'

'Well, that's something.'

'Why?'

'I don't like the way the girl looks at you,' said George, 'it's kind of embarrassing.'

'Too few men around, that's all,' said Toby. 'Now get this, George. I'm letting you come in with me, but you're not going to start anything this time. You're not going to say any of the bright things that come into your head. You're not going to get anyone drunk. You're just going to be there in the background, like a perfect little gentleman. I know the way I want to work things. Understand? Or do I have to shut you out on the door-step?'

'No,' said George, 'I'll just stick around.'

'Good, and don't forget yourself.' Toby parked the car and went on to ring the front-door bell of The Laurels and to ask for an interview with Mrs Milne.

She was in the sitting-room, sitting close to the fire, when the maid showed them in. She was wearing a black dress, close-fitting and long; against it her rings glittered with vivid reflections of the firelight. She looked up at them with a smile and rose. There was a quiet about her this afternoon, a stillness that was unfamiliar.

'Did you meet my daughter on your way here?' she asked when they were seated. 'Oh, she was going to the village, was she?' She made a soft sound that was perhaps a laugh. 'It's odd, you know, to remember that once it seemed quite easy to be a mother. One fed the child, and washed her, and dressed her, and called the doctor if she was ill, and tried to give her a nice time. But it's very difficult to decide the scope of one's responsibilities towards a more or less grown-up person. I've tried to interfere more, perhaps, than I ought. But now I've—I've decided to give in. I haven't told her yet, but I've decided.' She looked down at the fire with that same distant, introspective smile. 'At any rate,' she said, 'it's a peaceful feeling, giving in.'

'You've been trying to prevent her marriage, haven't you?' said Toby.

She nodded. 'She won't be happy if she marries

Adrian. She's a simple child really; she's got simple childish tastes, and her ideas are pretty childish and simple. And Adrian won't let that alone. He's already stopped her playing the jazz she really likes, and convinced her that she ought to be playing Chopin. He's injected psychological catchwords. He's trying to make her something she isn't capable of becoming. It'll exhaust her and fret her and end up by destroying her—if he isn't bored with her in a year, which is really the most probable thing.'

'And yet you've decided to give in.' Toby's eyes were keeping a thoughtful watch on hers.

'What else can one do?'

He shrugged.

'As a matter of fact,' she added, 'I don't really mean to let her marry till she's twenty-one, which is just about a year from now.' Then she gave him an amused look and said: 'I'm afraid I'm taking for granted that you're interested in my family affairs.'

'It's not a mistake,' he assured her. 'And now look at this.' He held out the anonymous letter.

She took it. She read it. She handed it back and looked him in the eyes.

Anna Milne's face was not one that betrayed much of what she was feeling or thinking. A minute or two ago it had expressed the calm, the satisfaction, almost, of resignation, and a sort of casual friendliness. Now a slight tightening of the muscles had wiped that out. It had become mask-like.

'This time,' she said, 'I don't understand.'

'I think I can explain—if,' said Toby with a sudden harshness in his voice, 'it's really necessary.'

'Please do,' she said.

He folded the piece of paper away in his pocket-book. 'You see,' he said, 'there's a pair of trousers missing in this case. Of course, you didn't know that.'

'No,' she said.

He smiled. 'All right, you didn't. But it—'

'Mr Dyke,' she cut in, 'if you're going to be rude to me you can drop out of this. The police can see that letter and deal with it as they think best. They'll do it, at least, without unnecessary insult.'

He leant forward and answered her earnestly: 'Look here, Mrs Milne, you're in a mess. You know it and you're frightened. What's more, you're worn out with being frightened. When you're worn out you make mistakes. You're making a mistake now. You ought to pool with me all that you know about those trousers. It's not an important mistake, because I think I know most of what it's necessary to know, but later on you'll find yourself making worse ones. Well, if I were you I'd guard against that by turning honest. Plant some of your trouble on me; I'm not going to be worn out for a long time yet.'

'How do I know,' she replied coldly, 'that you didn't write those letters to yourself?'

He sighed impatiently. 'There, that's what I mean. You'd never say a damnfool thing like that if you were in your right mind. If I knew enough to write myself these letters, I'd know enough to start blackmailing you right away—because that's what you're getting at, isn't it? I'd have no possible motive except blackmail.'

She dropped her eyes, drawing her hand across them. 'All right,' she said fretfully, 'I'm sorry. But please go on and tell me about the trousers. I want to understand.'

He said nothing for a moment. 'Very well,' he said then, 'we'll play it your way. You were at the inquest on the man who was killed, weren't you? Question luckily doesn't need an answer; I saw you there. Well, at the inquest a Mrs Quantick of Wallaford testified that he'd spent Monday night in her house. He left on Tuesday morning, carrying a suitcase. Presumably he'd meant to pack all his belongings and take them away with him, but somehow he managed to forget a jacket. It was a navy blue jacket, and he left it hanging in a cupboard in the room he'd slept in. In one of its pockets was Shelley Maxwell's passport, though that isn't what's important at the moment. What's important is that there was probably a pair of trousers belonging to that blue jacket, and if there was, those trousers must have been in the suitcase. Of course the jacket may have been an odd one; if I hadn't had this letter I don't suppose I should have started thinking about trousers at all. I know the trousers he was found in were tweed, and most people don't wear blue jackets with tweed trousers if they can help it, but I dare say some of them do, and, as I was saying, until I got this letter, I hadn't got trousers on my mind at all. But now I've been given this prod in that direction, I must say that the only significant pair of trousers I can think of are the ones that probably belonged to that blue jacket, and which are probably in the suitcase. In my opinion the probability is that there are other interesting things in the suitcase too, though that may be merely a romantic embroidery on the fact that the suitcase has disappeared. The police discovered that it was deposited in the station cloakroom in Wallaford on the Tuesday morning, but the next morning it was collected by some unidentified person, and since then it hasn't been seen. All we can get out of the cloakroom attendant about that person is that he was a tall, dark man with glasses. So far I haven't run into any tall, dark men with glasses connected with this case, and I'm making no guesses at who he is—'

'I'm ready to guess,' she interposed, 'that, whoever he is, he's the person who's been writing you these letters.'

'Possibly. Only what the second of these letters implies, if you haven't realized it yet, is that you're the person who's in possession of the suitcase. If you had the suitcase, if its contents were so dangerous to you that you had to burn them, then there was something about that accident on the Purbrook road that was different from anything that's come out about it yet. Don't you understand? Don't you see where this letter's trying to put you?'

She nodded. 'Of course I see. Someone's exercising a lot of ingenuity to get me arrested for the murder of Shelley Maxwell. That was obvious from the first letter. What I couldn't understand was what these mysterious truosers had to do with it. Now you've made that clear. As I see it, someone, probably this tall, dark man—by the way, do you ever wear glasses, Mr Dyke?—this someone, who of course knows where the trousers are, saw me making a bonfire the other afternoon, and thought what a clever thing it'd be to tell you it was these trousers I was burning. Don't you think—' she smiled at him—'he's got you sized up rather well? He seems to know just what sort of things you'll take seriously.'

Toby shifted irritably in his chair. 'Anyway,' he said, 'you *were* making a bonfire. I'm glad we haven't got to go round and round that too.'

'What d'you take me for?' she asked. 'Smoke goes up, doesn't it? Even a high laurel hedge doesn't conceal smoke. But, if you think about that for a moment, d'you think that if I'd wanted to destroy something secretly I should really have chosen as public a method as a bonfire?'

'The question is,' he replied, 'what's your story about what you actually did burn.'

'Autumn leaves,' she answered promptly. Then, at the look on his face, she burst out laughing. Toby laughed too. George, grave-faced, sat and watched them laughing at one another, she with a nervous helplessness, he with sardonically encouraging amusement.

'Oh, dear,' she said after a minute, wiping the hysterical tears away from her eyes, 'that was silly of me—and very rude to my gardener, if you think that we're well on into January. As a matter of fact, what I was burning—'

Toby stood up. 'If your sentences are going to begin with 'as a matter of fact' then I *know* there's no truth to be got out of you. And if it wasn't trousers you were burning—' he glared at her with a look of malevolence—'my dear Mrs Milne, *I don't care what it was!*'

Anna Milne and Toby Dyke looked at one another speculatively across the two or three feet that separated them.

Both of them had keen and intelligent faces, both had a grimness about the jaw, both were blatant in their curious study of one another.

Anna Milne smiled. 'Mr Dyke,' she said, 'please sit down. We haven't nearly finished our talk.'

He smiled too, indulgently. He answered: 'That needs demonstrating.'

'Very well,' she said, 'listen to this. Suppose I were to engage you to find the writer of these anonymous letters.'

His smile broadened. 'Just that?'

'Just that,' she said.

'The writer of the letters, nothing else at all?'

'I'm not interested in anything else.'

'Dear me,' said Toby.

'At any rate,' said Anna Milne, 'sit down.'

Toby started to walk about the room. His manner had become preoccupied, his black brows met above the beak of his nose. She watched him with a certain anxiety and with an obvious irritation at his movements.

After a moment she began hesitantly: 'The fee—'

'You leave the fee to Toby,' George advised her. 'He'll see it's big cnough.'

She rose suddenly and stood in Toby's way. They looked again into one another's faces.

'Mr Dyke—'

'Yes, it's a good idea in a way,' he answered. 'If you employ me I can make you do what I tell you. That's the correct relationship between employer and employee. And the first thing you'll do—' He stopped and said instead: 'My God, but you're scared, aren't you?'

She nodded.

'And if I ask you why, if I ask you to give me your confidence, if I waste any more time over the question-and-answer business, I'll get nothing out of you but tricks and dodges.'

She drew a difficult breath and said: 'It's unreasonable of me to be scared—I know that. But it's a horrible feeling, this—this malignity.'

'I repeat,' said Toby, 'if I ask, it will only be given me good and thick. Right. Then action's the thing. Come on, get your coat.'

'My—?'

'Coat,' said Toby, 'and hat, or anything else that'll come in handy when you're paying calls on people who've just been celebrating a funeral. No,' he went on quickly, as her eyes darkened and her lips curled back for a furious reply, 'I like my own rules best for this cut-throat game. I always turn up six cards in dummy before I start bidding.'

Toby refused to be driven in Mrs Milne's car. He also refused to drive her in the one he had hired. He pointed out that when they had concluded their visit to the Maxwells they might wish to go different ways. So it was with his car following hers that they approached Chovey Place.

In his seat beside Toby, George muttered half to himself: 'Now why? Why? You know all about that, I suppose. You know why she first says she thinks you're the cove who's been writing the letters, and then employs you to find out who he is—oh yes, you know all that! You know what you're playing at now too, oh yes, oh yes!'

'Her first manœuvre,' said Toby, 'was just an odd dodge for gaining time, on the old line that attack's the best method of defence. You know what Lord Baldwin said about that.'

'No,' said George.

'The second—'

'What did he say?'

'George, this is a serious matter, so serious that we can't afford to bring party politics into it. The second manœuvre, I was going to say, was most probably a dodge for keeping me under her eye. That doesn't mean she won't be glad if I find out who's actually been writing these letters, but it means—at least, she thinks it means—that she can do a bit of interfering when we start finding out some of the things she's keeping dark. She's crooked as a swastika, that woman. At least . . .'

'Eh?'

'Oh, hell, wipe out the crooked, and say she's one of the people who's dead sure that the end justifies the means.'

George grunted. 'And you're going along to Maxwells now because why?'

'Because it's the place she didn't want to go to. Wouldn't take us there this morning, would she?'

George grunted again. The blue eyes in the pink circle of his face were contemplative. He said nothing for a while. His next remark, when it came, was: 'Tobe, she's mighty attached to that daughter of hers, shouldn't you say? A very loving mother, eh?'

'Yes—and yet thinks she's a fool.'

'Nothing in that,' said George authoritatively.

He was silent again. He was absent-mindedly smoothing the palms of his hands against one another; he was also sucking at his teeth, producing little chirps of sound.

When Toby pulled his car up behind Mrs Milne's outside the wrought-iron gates of Chovey Place, remarking that Adrian Laws must still be at the house since his three-wheeler was still parked there, it was George who got out and opened the gates. When both cars stopped again a few minutes later in front of the house, it was George who was out first and setting a thick finger, tipped with a dirty fingernail, firmly on the bell.

'And now that we're here,' said Mrs Milne, as they waited for the door to open, 'what do we do?'

'You show them the letter,' said Toby.

'And?'

'Oh, you just show it.'

'But that'll imply I think that they've got something to do with it,' she said sharply.

Toby grinned.

She took a step towards her car. 'Mr Dyke, you may be a—'

The door opened. Toby started explaining to the butler that Mrs Milne had called to see Sir Joseph and Lady Maxwell about a most urgent matter. She returned to his side. From that moment on she showed no further reluctance or indecision; indeed, when the door of the drawing-room was opened for them, she entered the room with a manner that was both assured and formidable.

The Maxwells were all there, having tea. Sir Joseph and his brother, so the butler had informed them as they were crossing the hall, had just returned from the funeral. Stuart Maxwell was standing to one side of the fire, an elbow on the mantelpiece. His face had a blanched, unusually flabby look. His gaze on Anna Milne was bewildered, almost stricken.

On the settee before the fire sat Lady Maxwell, still with her fur wrap round her shoulders. Adrian sat beside her. On her face there appeared surprise and pleasure, on his a curious, smooth blankness, behind which lurked secretive, malicious amusement. As his eyes met Toby's one eyelid, without actually dropping, seemed to tense itself significantly behind the horn-rimmed lense.

Sir Joseph was sitting at a slight distance from the others. He sat near an open window, a cup of extremely weak tea on a table at his side. He had a lettuce-leaf in one hand and a slice of brown bread and butter in the other.

At sight of the visitors he crammed the lettuce-leaf into his mouth, moved in one long stride to the french window, opened it, stepped outside and shut it again behind him. Through the glass his large, yellowish face, his beard and his spidery length, showed against the deep shadows of the afternoon twilight with a patchiness that was eerily unpleasant.

'Joseph!' Sunk in her corner of the couch, Lady Maxwell was trying to jerk herself up on to her feet. Her blue eyes were furious, her lips munched against one another.

But Mrs Milne had not waited for her. Only a moment after Sir Joseph, she crossed the room and flung the window open.

She was cool, almost assertively cool.

'Sir Joseph,' she said, 'you're a damned humbug.'

He had already retreated a pace or two.

'You can't bolt off like that,' she said loudly, 'as if you'd a genuine grief to excuse you. If I believed you were suffering from grief I shouldn't have come here. I've come here to show you something. If you walk off across the park I'll come too and see that you get a look at it before I leave you. Grief!' She laughed. In speaking her voice had been level, but in her laugh it betrayed her; it quivered, like a taut string, with anger.

'Grief?' he echoed. 'I hadn't thought—no, certainly I hadn't thought—of offering that as an explanation of my leaving the room when you entered it.' He spoke abruptly, nervously; one hand was fidgeting at the corner of a pocket. It was an arresting voice, and the angular figure with the cold eyes set far apart in the big face, was striking in its aloof, nervous dignity.

'I left the room,' he continued, 'simply because I had no wish to speak with you, nor with your—friends. I am not a humbug. I have always made my attitude towards you perfectly clear. Now please allow me to go. This must be very unpleasant for the others who are present.'

'Joseph!' cried his wife again, but was too filled with emotion to say what she wanted to say. She was standing, her small hands tightly clenched together. There was fury on her face, but also the abjectness of keen humiliation.

Stuart Maxwell's pallid face had flushed. It flushed blotchily, making him look ill. In a slurred voice that sounded dangerous, he said: 'You're an unmannered dog, Joe, you're a hypocrite, one day I'll kill you.'

Mrs Milne, still with that cool, angry control of herself, held out the anonymous letter to Sir Joseph.

'This,' she said, 'is what I came to show you. When you've seen it you can go or stay, so far as I'm concerned.'

He took the letter, coming into the room and shutting the window behind him. The room had been growing exceedingly cold while it was open, but he seemed to have no awareness of temperature.

'Well?' he said when he had read the letter. 'Well?'

'Do you understand it?' she asked.

'Possibly, in part.'

'You do?' she said, on a sharp note of surprise.

'Please, Anna, may I see it too?' said Lady Maxwell.

Mrs Milne took it from Sir Joseph and handed it to his wife, but her attention did not leave him for an instant. There was irony in his small, cold eyes. He almost smiled.

'*I* can't understand it at *all*,' said Lady Maxwell. 'Do you really understand it, Joseph, or—?'

'Or,' said the major, who had taken the letter from her and read it too, 'is brother Joe refusing, as usual, to admit when he's stumped?'

'If you had considered the evidence we possess,' said Sir Joseph, 'this letter—'

Mrs Milne cut in: 'This letter, you would realize, accuses me of murder. It's the second of the kind I've had. Someone in this village is exercising an astonishing amount of ingenuity in an attempt to make it seem that I worked that accident the other night deliberately.'

'Anna!' And turning suddenly to Toby, Lady Maxwell said: 'Mr Dyke, I'm quite, quite at sea. Won't you please explain? Anna can't mean what she's just said.'

In a grave voice Sir Joseph announced: 'This must be given to the police.'

'Certainly,' said Mrs Milne.

'The police,' he continued, 'will take a serious view of it.'

'They will!'

'You should have taken it to the police at once,' he said.

'I preferred,' she said, 'to bring it here.'

'You believe I can assist you in some way?'

She turned to Toby with the smile that could flash so brilliantly over her face. 'I like it, don't you,' she said, 'when he turns into the grave magistrate, the worthy adviser? Do I think you can assist me, Joe? Well, that depends. I can assist you, I think. I can explain that the police are asking me over and over again one question—*one* question. Is there anyone, they want to know, who's got a grudge against me?'

'Well?' he said.

'So far I haven't answered them. But if there's one person in this neighbourhood who's never hesitated to show his dislike of me, or to take any opportunity that offered to make trouble for me—'

'Oh, Anna,' cried Lady Maxwell, 'no one in this neighbourhood dislikes you. Nobody could. Everyone admires you—I know they do.'

'Except,' said Anna Milne, 'your own "prating fool", as you call him.'

'My—?'

Lady Maxwell stopped. She gasped faintly. Her husband, sitting down and crossing one bony knee over the other, remarked: 'So that's what you call me, is it, Emmie?'

She was working her lips together, her blue eyes filled with a deep surprise. He smiled. There were chips of ice in his smile.

' "Prating fool." Indeed,' he murmured, 'indeed.'

'But—' she said, 'but I don't—'

A short, harsh, uncomfortable laugh broke from Mrs Milne, and she looked at Toby Dyke. 'Why the hell,' she said venomously, 'did you bring me here?'

'You needn't stay,' he replied.

'Thanks,' she said ironically. Then harshly, defensively, to Lady Maxwell: 'I'm sorry, Emmeline, that was unforgivable of me. I don't know how I came to say it. This whole thing's damnably on my mind. I don't believe I'm quite sane at the moment.'

'Oh,' said Lady Maxwell in a quick, gentle voice, 'I don't mind. It's only that I'm puzzled. I can't understand how . . . But I don't *mind*. I'm never in the least ashamed of my opinions.'

'No, indeed,' said her husband, 'Emmeline never makes any secret of her opinion of me. You needn't concern yourself, Mrs Milne, nor exercise yourself with an unaccustomed delicacy. Emmeline herself is quite without delicacy in certain directions—for instance, the matter of our son's death. She's acted in such a way as to make all our acquaintances terrified of meeting us. For she so forces her own singular view of the circumstances upon them that they're forced either into an insincere pandering to her delusions, or else into showing their doubts of her sanity. I shall not blame them if they completely avoid us in the future.'

Lady Maxwell did not appear to have heard him. She said: 'And I'm still very puzzled. What I cannot understand is—'

Mrs Milne interrupted her by once more addressing Toby Dyke. 'I hope,' she said, 'you've got what you came for. As I've your permission to go, I'm going. Emmeline, I'm sincerely sorry. But we'll talk it over another time, shall we? Goodbye.' For a moment, before she went, her eyes met Stuart Maxwell's. It was the only time during the visit that she appeared to be aware of his presence.

She had given no sign in her abrupt withdrawal of whether or not she expected Toby and George to follow her. Toby's attention was on Lady Maxwell, and it was clear that, for a moment at least, he intended to stay behind.

'You were saying . . . ?' he remarked.

'Yes, that it's a most puzzling . . .'

'Perhaps,' he said, 'I might be able to help explain . . .'

She took the suggestion thoughtfully. 'Perhaps,' she said slowly, 'you could.' And she smiled at him, as if they had just been making an arrangement.

A contemptuous sound came from Sir Joseph. 'Fortunately,' he said, 'this house is my property. I do not invite either of these reporters, these sensation-hunters, to remain. Can't you perceive, Emmie, that what they want from you is the biggest exhibition of yourself that you're capable of making?'

'If it's making an exhibition of myself,' she replied, 'to assert a simple fact against the ridiculous and perverted view which you have forced on people, deceiving them and—'

'For God's sake,' said Major Maxwell, 'if that's starting again, let's get out.' And grabbing Toby by the elbow, he pushed him out into the hall. George and Adrian followed them.

*

Adrian was the first person Toby addressed.

'Well,' he said, 'you enjoyed that, didn't you?'

Adrian was thrusting both hands through his copper-coloured hair. The smile on his face expressed a quiet satisfaction of spirit.

'Yes,' he admitted, 'I did.'

'Scenes and such-like,' said Toby, 'you appreciate them.'

'Although, of course,' said Adrian, 'the best's only beginning now.'

'Oh, quite,' said Toby.

Adrian stood still in the middle of the big, barren hall.

'What are you looking at me like that for?' he demanded.

'So's to get you anxious and asking questions,' said Toby. 'Most people around here are pretty anxious about one thing or another, seems to me.'

'No, but really—'

'Well, you did something pretty funny in there, don't you?'

'I didn't do a thing.'

'Not a thing,' Toby agreed. He turned to the major. 'Come to think of it, you'd do pretty well as a suspect, wouldn't you?'

The major's jaw set sullenly. 'What d'you mean, suspect?' He said it with a heavy dullness that did not sit upon him too convincingly.

'He means,' said Adrian, amused, 'that he thinks you're the one who's been sending Anna those threatening letters.'

'No,' said Stuart Maxwell, and all at once his features were taut, his eyes, for all their weariness, were keen, and he looked more like himself. 'No, Adrian, don't be fooled. Go on, Dyke.'

'Well, suppose,' said Toby, 'suppose for the sake of

interest, of argument, and, just remotely possibly, of truth, that the hints in those letters are not totally, entirely without foundation. Suppose, that's to say, that murder isn't an utterly fantastic suggestion . . .'

'Ah,' said the major, with a sort of sigh that sounded, oddly enough, relieved, 'at last somebody's said it. Murder. Thanks, Dyke. There's just a hope now of getting somewhere. Murder. Good. I don't like this edging around things. Murder, murder, murder!' The last time he said it it was almost a shout, and then his voice cracked into sudden laughter.

'Here, steady on, old man,' said Adrian. 'I know this is all pretty damnable for you—worse than for the rest of us, but—'

The older man turned on him. 'Get out,' he said, 'I want to talk to Dyke.'

'But—'

'Get out!' Then his tone changed. He said: 'Sorry, Adrian. I don't mean it like that. But I want to talk to Dyke. You don't mind clearing out for a bit, do you?'

'I want to talk to him myself,' said Adrian, 'some time.' He looked vexed. But, shrugging his shoulders, he wandered off down the drive.

George, watching him go, observed: 'And Lady Maxwell wants to talk to you, Tobe, and so, I shouldn't wonder, does Sergeant Eggbear. This is what I call no sort of holiday.'

'It isn't a holiday any longer, it's work,' Toby reminded him. 'I'm employed now.'

'What's that?' said the major quickly.

'Mrs Milne's employed me to find the letter-writer. But let's forget the letter-writer for the moment, and go back to—'

'Ah yes, to the murder. You think I make a good suspect?'

They were standing now beside the old Sunbeam.

Toby was lighting a cigarette. Round the flame his shrewd eyes studied the other man. George remarked: 'Kind of a hero, ain't he, Tobe?'

'Yes,' said Toby, 'kind of. If there's talk of murder, you're all for having it directed at you, aren't you, major? Seems that the rumours I've heard about the decay of chivalry are all bunk. Unless of course—'

'Unless what?' said Maxwell.

'Unless you just think you'd like to keep the police on the hop for a bit, knowing that when you feel like it you can pop out with some nice watertight proof of how it couldn't have been you. However, let's go into the possibilities where you're concerned. Because obviously Mrs Milne isn't the only person who could have committed the murder. She did the killing with her car, there doesn't seem to be much doubt of that. But the murderer, if there was one, was the person who got the drunk man to lie down in the right place. May have been her, or may have been anyone else who happened to be around—and who, of course, carried away with him that bottle we hunted for so busily the other day. And there's no denying that you're a good candidate for that vacancy.'

'Just so,' said the major. 'I live very close, I'd have recognized Shelley, I've got whisky on my premises. But you want a motive, don't you?'

'Badly.'

'Well, I've got one.'

'Inheritance?'

Maxwell nodded.

Toby chuckled. 'Almost too pretty to be real, isn't it? And then there are your various—um, lies.'

'Yes,' said Maxwell. 'I can explain them, of course, only—'

Toby raised a questioning eyebrow.

'Only,' said Maxwell, 'I don't know how good a story the explanation makes. Which lies, by the way, do you want explained?'

'I'd like to know,' said Toby, 'why you told the police you went straight home when Mrs Milne dropped you on the way back from the badminton match. Because her car stopped opposite the stile, didn't it, for a goodish time? —long enough for quite a lot of oil to drip on the road. And why did you make up the tarradiddle about looking along the road and seeing the lights of a car? Because, if you *had* looked along the road and seen the lights of a car, you'd also have seen, and later you'd have remembered, the bridge, which would have blotted out anyone walking along the road beyond it.'

'Ye-es,' said Stuart Maxwell, 'I suppose that's so. Didn't strike me, but you're quite right. It isn't particularly important though. But the other bit—well, I had to say it, to corroborate Mrs Milne's story. You see, what actually happened was this. At the end of the match Mrs Milne gave me and Miss Willis a lift home. Miss Willis lives a little way down the main road. Mrs Milne dropped me at the crossroads, we said good night, and I started home. But I waited at the stile. When she came by after dropping Miss Willis I stepped out and stopped her. I'd intended, you see, to use the drive home to ask her to marry me. I hadn't expected Miss Willis. And having got myself to the point, it was too much of an anticlimax just to let the thing slip by. See what I mean? So I waited and got down to it. We talked, I should think, for about ten minutes. I got a pretty definite refusal. Well, that was that, and I went home. Incidentally, all the time I was standing there—and altogether it must have been about twenty minutes—nobody passed me in either direction. That was why I went to the trouble of inventing the story about the car. I didn't see why the police shouldn't have the information they wanted, the perfectly accurate information, that nobody had passed. But as I was supposed to have gone straight home I had to make up something to explain how I could be so certain.'

'I see,' said Toby.

'I'm not worrying much,' said the major, 'about whether or not you're believing me.'

'That,' said Toby, 'is one thing at least that I don't believe. But go on.'

'Well, for myself, I'd have had nothing against telling the truth about all this straight away, but I couldn't do that without contradicting Mrs Milne's story. I'd no idea at the time, of course, how serious it was going to turn out to be. But what happened was this. When the police asked Mrs Milne about her movements on the Tuesday night, she decided to leave out the bit about our conversation. Her object was merely to save me embarrassment, nothing more. She told them that when she'd dropped Miss Willis she drove straight back, until she was held up by that sports car coming over the bridge. Heard anything about that car yet, by the way?'

Toby shook his head. 'Though they go on asking for it on the wireless, I believe.'

'Well, having modified the truth in this manner,' the major went on, 'she rang me up as soon as she knew the police intended to check up on me and told me her story and asked me to stick to it. So when the constable turned up here I was all prepared—too prepared, I'm afraid; I don't think I acted surprise at the accident quite as well as I ought to have done. Anyhow, there are all the facts for you, and you can make what you like of them.'

'On the contrary,' said Toby, 'I shall have to let them make what they like of me. Still, I'm glad to know. Mind if it all gets handed on to Eggbear?'

The major hesitated, then said: 'No, I don't mind.'

'Thanks. Then George and I'll be getting back to Chovey.'

They got into the car. The major waited until they had started, then turned away in the direction of his cottage.

George sank low down upon the seat, closed his eyes and said that he could do with a nice cup of tea. Toby agreed absentmindedly.

After a few minutes George remarked: 'You know, I like driving in the dark. Kind of soothing. I like the way the telephone-poles jump out at you.'

'George,' said Toby, 'you've got a nose. You've got a way of knowing things without exactly being told. What d'you think of that story?'

'D'you mean,' said George drowsily, 'do I believe it?'

'Do you?'

'Well, you know, Tobe,' said George, 'I'm a trusting enough soul myself, but when I'm with you I pick up the habit of expecting even the hall umbrella-stand to tell me lies. So I reckon I'm spoilt for your present purpose.'

CHAPTER 10

'Sam,' said Toby, 'have you ever heard of a Mrs Langman?'

'No,' said the sergeant.

'Sure?' said Toby.

'Yes,' said the sergeant.

'Say,' said George, 'is there any way of making this stove give out a little heat?'

Eggbear heaved himself on to his feet, went to the stove, opened it at the top and looked inside. 'Yes,' he said, 'you could relight it.' He slumped back into his chair, picked up a pencil and started chewing the india-rubber at the end of it.

Toby's face was patient. 'So you haven't heard of a Mrs Langman?'

'No,' grunted Eggbear. 'When did you?'

'Recently. She's the sister of Mrs Milne's cook.'

'What about her?'

'I was just thinking you could save me a bit of trouble if—'

'Eh?' said the sergeant. 'I could save you some trouble, could I? How nice. I could save you—' He broke off and tittered sardonically. 'You're savin' me a lot of trouble, I suppose? You're makin' everythin' nice and easy for me? I should think so! Why, if you'd not been along this way, would anyone have written you anonymous letters? I ask you, would they? 'Tis you bein' here that's put the notion in somebody's head. People like you are always puttin' notions where they don't belong. 'Tis all along of you—'

'Listen,' said Toby, 'there's something I want done. I want you to send someone round to Mrs Langman, of this address—' and he handed over the envelope on the back of which he had noted down the address that Ruby Leat had given him—'and get him to find out why, in the opinion of Mrs Langman and her sister, Mrs Milne is beyond the pale. And tell him not to be put off with stories of unmentionable sins; I want my revelations concrete.'

'What's it all about?' said Eggbear, frowning and running the tip of his pencil up and down the corrugations on his forehead. 'All this you been tellin' me about what you been up to today, and now this . . . D'you know what what you'm talkin' about, Toby, or are you just throwin' things all around you like, and waitin' to see what comes back?'

'A few of the things I've thrown around have already come back, Sam. You see, in my opinion—'

'Tobe,' said George, 'would you mind telling me if we're going to be remaining in this ice-box more than a minute or two, or shall I relight the sergeant's stove, like he says?'

'It's all right, we're just going,' said Toby. 'You see, Sam, in my opinion this village of yours is a very unhealthy spot. Maybe mortally unhealthy. And you are, so to speak, its medical officer. I should hate to see you fail in serious realization of your responsibilities.'

Eggbear whistled. 'But look here, that letter you shown me today, and that other . . .'

But Toby had gone to the door. 'We'll be in the bar this evening if you've anything to tell us about that Mrs Langman. So long, Sam.'

Eggbear found himself alone. He sat there, chewing fiercely on his indiarubber.

In the bar of the Ring of Bells, George and Toby, over their beer, talked with Tom Warren of horses, dogs and football. Not a single corpse was mentioned, not a single anonymous letter. But after about twenty minutes someone called Tom Warren away, and when he came back it was to tell Toby that Lady Maxwell was in the vestibule, wanting to speak with him.

Toby gulped his drink.

'Where can I take her?' he asked.

'Drawing-room upstairs'll be empty,' said Tom Warren, 'and there's a nice fire.'

'Thanks. Come on George.' And Toby hurried out.

Upstairs, amongst the bulrushes in tall, painted vases, the velvet-framed pictures of nymphs, the mirrors, the green and pink rugs and the deal-stained-mahogany furniture of Tom's refined drawing-room, Lady Maxwell hurried into explanations of why she had come. Beside the nice fire she unbuttoned her sealskin coat; she put her small feet on the brass fender. Eagerness made her face look oddly young.

'I felt I had to come, Mr Dyke, the *moment* I could get away,' she said. 'I felt you would be certain to want some explanations from me. I felt I owed them to you. So as soon as Harvey was free—I don't like to interrupt his work, you see, he really has such a lot to do, and is so good about it—just as soon as he was free I got him to drive me here. And I mustn't be long, because I don't think it's fair to keep him. Well, I feel I ought to explain that strange little incident this afternoon—not explain it, that's to say, because I can't. What I'm hoping is that you may be able to explain it to me. But I can at least explain to you why I was so deeply, so profoundly puzzled by what may have seemed to you quite a commonplace little incident.'

'You mean by Mrs Milne's accusing you of calling your husband a prating fool?' said Toby. 'I've heard husbands called worse things than that.'

'Oh, I hope you have, Mr Dyke, for of course many of them deserve far worse things than my husband. But you see, this is why I was so bewildered: I have only once used that particular expression about him. Only once. I'm quite positive of that. And that once was—well, I cannot understand by what possible means Anna Milne could have knowledge of it.'

'Would you mind telling me?'

She lifted a hand to shield her face from Tom Warren's generous fire. 'That's why I'm here. Mr Dyke, I've told you of my relations with my son. You've seen some of his letters. For each of those letters I must have written three or four to him. In fact, I've written at least once a week ever since he went away. And with my weekly letter I nearly always sent him a copy of our local paper. I knew he'd like to be kept in touch with what was going on. Just our little local events, you know, that no other paper would notice. He wrote to me that he always looked forward very much to receiving it. Well, in one copy of the paper there was a report, a very long and dull report, I'm afraid, of a speech my husband had made to the local branch of the League of Nations Union. Dear, dear, such a very long and very dull speech I found it, though that may just have been my own very personal reaction, and not at all a fair criticism, since, naturally, all its contents were familiar to me. I had heard my husband say everything in it a great many times before. Of course, I suppose that people who do a great deal of public speaking can't help repeating themselves, unless they have very original minds. But you see, I had argued with my husband over a number of points in his speech, offered thoughtful criticisms, and had found that my view was totally disregarded. So you can understand that when I had to listen to yet another repetition of his too, too familiar fallacies, my state of mind became definitely censorious. Then when I read the report in the paper, taking up nearly two and a half columns, well—' She gave a little titter. 'Out came my silver pencil, a present from Shelley at least twenty years ago, and I wrote in the margin: "The wise in heart will receive commandments, but the prating fool shall fail." Then I put the paper in the envelope with my letter and posted it. Now—' Her earnest eyes widened with excitement. 'Now how did Anna Milne know about that?'

Toby balanced, the poker, which he had picked up during her story, across two outstretched fingers. 'You're dead sure she couldn't have seen it before you stuck it in the envelope?'

'But of course. I was in my drawing-room, sitting at my bureau. There was no one else in the room.'

'Who posted the letter?'

'I posted it myself. I've always posted all my letters to my son. I wasn't anxious that anyone should know I was in such regular communication with him.'

'Ah yes.' Toby rolled the poker backwards and forwards along his fingers. 'How long ago was this?'

'Only about two months. Quite recently. The details are all fresh in my mind.'

Toby nodded. He tucked his upper lip between his teeth and chewed it thoughtfully.

'Very interesting. And you're dead sure—' this came abruptly—'that you haven't used that "prating fool" expression any other time? I mean, there are some expressions one uses all the time without being in the least aware of it.'

But she repeated firmly that she was perfectly sure.

Toby turned to George. 'I'm beginning to feel pretty certain,' he said, 'where that suitcase is.'

'That's right,' said George.

'What d'you mean?' said Lady Maxwell. 'Do you understand it? Do you know where the paper is?'

'Reckon it's burnt,' said George.

'You see,' said Toby, 'if you've really used that expression only the once, then Mrs Milne must have seen the paper on which you wrote it. If you posted it without any possibility of her having seen it before it went to South Africa, then, unless someone she knows there—'

Lady Maxwell interrupted: 'She often told me she's completely lost touch with all her acquaintances there. I think she was glad to, you know; I don't think she was at all happy there.'

'There's no special reason to believe everything she says,' said Toby. 'But as I was saying, unless someone she knows there thought it worth while to write and tell her that you thought your husband a prating fool, then she must have seen the paper after it came back from South Africa.'

'After it came *back*?'

'It came back, I should imagine,' said Toby, 'in the suitcase of the man who was run over. The suitcase that's missing at present. The suitcase that was collected the morning after the murder—'

'The—?' She caught the word back with a shrill gasp. Her hands flew up to her mouth.

Toby sprang up. 'I'm sorry, I'm awfully sorry. That's the trouble about having a sensational mind. The morning after the *accident* is of course what I meant to say.'

Her stiffened body relaxed in her chair but her face

remained blanched. When Toby continued there was a look in her eyes as if she were scarcely listening to him.

'The suitcase that was collected the morning after the *accident*,' he said, 'by a tall, dark man with glasses. That anonymous letter Mrs Milne showed you today was trying to make us believe that the suitcase is in Mrs Milne's possession. I didn't know in the least whether or not to believe it. Now I do believe it. At least . . .'

He looked at her speculatively, but it was obvious that she had no idea of what he had been saying. As if his ceasing to speak, however, were a sign for her to leave, she got to her feet a little staggeringly.

'Thank you, Mr Dyke, thank you so very much for listening to me so patiently. I hope I shall see you again. I've found the talks we've had so interesting.'

She wandered uncertainly to the door.

But suddenly she paused, and all at once was self-possessed.

'Mr Dyke, you said murder. Is that indeed what you believe?'

He shrugged his shoulders.

She went on evenly: 'Because, if it is, I would like you, I would beg you, to drop all investigation and go home. Leave it. Leave circumstances to work themselves out in their own way. I implore you most earnestly, go home.'

'That's what I have been wanting him to do ever since we came here,' said George.

Toby replied: 'I suppose you know it's a funny-sounding thing to ask.'

She nodded. 'Yes, yes. Mr Dyke, I'm certain you're a most brilliant and intelligent man. If there has in fact been a murder, if you search for the murderer, I know you will find him. You will find him and deliver him to the law. You will offer him up helpless to the gallows. Oh, please, please, I beg you, go home. Think of it — the gallows. Yes, I understand perfectly how strange this may sound. Some people might even take serious exception to my attitude. Not that I've ever paid much attention to appearances, or to what others think of me. And, you see, I am utterly, most convincedly, with the whole strength of my mind and spirit, with the whole of me—yes, and I belong to every society that is working to that end, even to those in foreign countries—I am completely and unrelentingly against the abominable crime of capital punishment!'

'And what,' said George, when they had had their supper, 'does the brilliant and intelligent bloke sitting opposite me mean to do about it?'

Toby pushed back his flopping lock of black hair with a rather weary hand. 'D'you know, I don't know that it's such a bad idea, going home,' he said.

'Except,' said George, 'that you happen to have taken on a job. Don't you go spoiling the atmosphere of confidence between you and your employer. Now myself, I want to think about it.'

Toby stretched himself, blowing smoke at the ceiling. He was lying flat on his back diagonally across the flowered quilt on the double bed in his room. They had gone up there to avoid the friendly company downstairs.

'Would you say,' said Toby, 'that that woman was a quick thinker?'

'Her ladyship?' said George. 'Well, you never know, but if it turned out she was, I'll admit it'd give me a considerable turn.'

'Yes,' said Toby, 'but if she were . . . You see what a bad position that story of hers puts Mrs Milne in. It's a very neat corroboration of the flannel-trousers letter. If it's true, it suggests that our letter-writer really knows a thing or two and isn't just using his deductive powers to a somewhat imaginative end. It means Mrs Milne must have the suitcase—or must have had it, because, of course, the bonfire may have made a convenient end to a number of things. If it isn't true . . . But if it isn't, it means that Lady Maxwell saw the possibilities of that "prating fool" remark damn quickly, because I'll swear she started gasping her bewilderment and acting peculiarly the very moment the remark was out. Even if she didn't think of all the details on the spot, she must have seen the rough outlines like a flash of lightning. And somehow I find it difficult to believe that her mind can tick along even as fast as most other people's.'

'I want,' said George, 'to have a quiet little think about that suitcase.'

'Do you? What I'm doing the quieter kind of thinking about at the moment,' said Toby, 'is that tall, dark man with glasses. There are three tall men in this case. One's dark, but he's got a beard. The cloakroom attendant wouldn't have forgotten to mention a beard. One wears glasses, but he's red-haired. One doesn't wear glasses and hasn't got dark hair either—hasn't had it, that's to say, for a good number of years. I'm rather wondering whether the only bits of that description which would apply to that individual once he was well away from the cloakroom are the "tall" and the "man". You can't disguise height, and it isn't usually easy to disguise sex.'

'My quiet think,' said George, 'is going to be really quiet. I'm going for a stroll. While I'm gone—' he put a hand inside his jacket—'you may as well take a look at these.' And he tossed something down on the bed beside Toby.

Without sitting up Toby reached for it and held it up to examine it.

'Christ!' he said. 'Hey, George—'

But George had gone out, closing the door behind him.

What Toby held was a few sheets of paper, folded into a wad. At a glance it had been easy to recognize the writing on the paper as that of Shelley Maxwell. Sorting out the sheets, Toby found that there were three letters; one was the first of the two written to Lady Maxwell with Shelley's left hand, the second, to make a guess from its date, was the letter that must have immediately preceded it, the third was one that had been written about three months later. Toby sat up suddenly and carried them to the light.

He spent a long time looking at the letters. But George took even longer to have his quiet think about the suitcase. After the first hour Toby went down to see whether the thinking might be taking place in front of a dart-board or over a game of skittles. But George was not in the bar. Returning to his room, Toby smoked cigarettes without stopping, and alternated minutes spent flat on his back with minutes of furious walking around the furniture.

When at last, without the warning of any step on the stair, George slipped quietly in and sat down by the fire, Toby's nerves were so strung with impatience that he jumped as if a cracker had gone off under his feet.

'Where the hell have you been?' he demanded.

'Just walking and thinking,' said George. He held out chubby hands to the fire.

Toby thrust the letters out to him. 'Where did you get these?' he rapped out.

'Why, didn't you see?' said George. 'I took them this morning when I was tying the packet up all nice and tidy to hand back to the old lady. You ain't very good with your eyes, are you, Tobe?'

Toby slumped down in the wicker chair opposite him.

'Anyway, you were perfectly right about them,' he said. 'The third one's a forgery.'

'That's what I thought,' said George.

'So's the second, of course. He wrote with his left hand, making up the story about having hurt his right, so's to hide the fact that he hadn't got the knack of Maxwell's writing yet. That accounts, incidentally, for the lack of any scar on his finger.'

'There was another letter written with his left hand some time later,' said George.

'Yes, I imagine he was wanting extra money to get back to England. The last time he said he was hurt he got a remittance rather above the usual, so he probably just tried it on again. And it worked.'

George nodded. 'And what are you going to do about it?'

Toby turned to the earliest of the letters, the one whose genuineness he had not questioned.

'I'm going to cable,' he said, 'to the police in the place where this letter was written from, to ask whether anyone called Maxwell died at this address some time between these two dates, May the nineteenth and June the eleventh—and if so, who were the friends that buried him.'

George was looking meditatively at the fire. 'Are you by any chance expecting,' he asked, 'that the name will be Milne?'

'I am not,' said Toby, 'any more than I expect it to be Bartlemy.'

A log crashed out of the fire. George's feet shot out of the way, but he picked the log up with his hands and jerked it back on to the flames.

'Well,' he said, 'I've worked out about that suitcase.'

'You've what?'

'Worked out where the suitcase is. Mrs Milne's got it.'

'Indeed. Mrs Milne's got it. You've worked it out.'

'Yes,' said George, with a hint of defensiveness in his manner, as Toby, leaning back in the wicker chair, regarded him with irony, 'I reasoned it out to my own satisfaction. If you ain't satisfied, you ain't. But me, I shall go on on the supposition that Mrs Milne is in possession of that suitcase.'

'George,' said Toby, 'quit telling lies. How did you get in?'

George chuckled. 'French window round at the side. The catch was a crime; I could've forced it with my eyelashes. All the same, Tobe, I did reason it out: I reasoned it out that if Mrs Milne had ever had the suitcase she'd probably got it still, because it was a leather suitcase, you see, Tobe. You can get a pair of trousers destroyed in a bonfire, and papers are easy if there aren't too many of 'em, but a leather suitcase'd be pretty near impossible. So I says to myself that if it isn't all someone's imagination the suitcase is probably still in the house, and the least suspicious place for a suitcase in a house is the box-room, if there is one. So I went along out and—'

'George,' said Toby seriously, 'I know this is all in the cause of science, but another time no housebreaking without my permission. I don't feel certain that you'll always choose your occasions so—justifiably.'

'Sure, Tobe, I know just how you feel. Well, I got in by the side, and went upstairs. The daughter was playing the piano, so I hardly had to trouble about walking quiet. I just went up to the top floor and started opening doors till I found the right one. Sort of an attic with a skylight. There was trunks and hatboxes and Gladstone bags and quite a number of leather suitcases, but the stuff on top didn't have to be worried about; I went straight for the stuff in behind. And there it was in a corner, behind a Saratoga trunk and a couple of picnic hampers. A leather suitcase with the initials SM.'

CHAPTER 11

Sunday was a day of rest. Very little happened. Eggbear let Toby know that he had discovered that his wife knew Lucy Langman, and believed she had an inkling of what the quarrel between Mrs Milne and her cook had been about. At any rate, Mrs Eggbear was going over to Purbrook today to visit her mother, and would look in on the Langmans and see if she could get the whole story out of them.

Toby and George themselves went into Wallaford. They dispatched a cable, had lunched at the Palace Hotel and went to the pictures. Wallaford, subsisting largely on holiday-makers, was naturally a centre of Sabbath-breaking; from one o'clock on there were seven cinemas to choose amongst. They returned to dinner at the Ring of Bells, and afterwards George beat everyone who would play with him at skittles. Adrian Laws and Daphne Milne dropped into the bar for a short time and had a couple of drinks on Toby. Daphne was silent, making unnecessary little nervous gestures with her hands and avoiding Toby's gaze; no matter how constantly or how admiringly he kept it upon her, she would not respond to it. Adrian was full of gossip, sufficiently amusing, but there was nothing in it to interest Toby.

Only, as they were going, Daphne suddenly came back from the door to say: 'Mr Dyke, will you be coming to see my mother tomorrow?'

'I might,' said Toby, 'but I should think the day after's more likely.'

She hesitated. 'If I wanted to talk to you tomorrow or — or any time, would I find you here?'

Outside there was a roaring sound as Adrian succeeded in getting his three-wheeler cranked up.

'Yes,' said Toby, 'and tomorrow wouldn't be a bad time to come and talk to me — would it?'

'Perhaps. I think I — perhaps . . .'

But though Toby stayed in the whole of the next day, Daphne Milne did not appear.

It was late on the Monday evening that he received the answer to his cable. It ran: 'Shelley Maxwell died here in hospital appendicitis May thirtieth friend Henry Rhymer stated he had no relatives undertook burial Rhymer's present whereabouts unknown.'

With this cable Toby and George called on the Eggbears.

Mrs Eggbear had been just about to go to bed, in fact the first curler was already in her hair when the doorbell rang. But she insisted on putting the kettle on to make tea, and on talking so hard whenever Toby tried to explain to the sergeant why they had come that Toby relapsed into irritated silence. Even when he tried asking her how she got on with Mrs Langman in Purbrook she was chattering of other things so busily that his question was lost.

But that spurred Toby on. He repeated it.

When he had repeated it a third time it began to be apparent that it was precisely that question which Mrs Eggbear was working so hard to avoid answering.

Her husband yawned over his teacup.

'Oh, get on and tell him,' he said, 'he'll give you no peace till you do.'

'But 'tis not the sort of thing that's of the slightest interest to you, Mr Dyke,' she said, her face flushing with embarrassment.

'You never know,' said Toby.

'I do know,' she replied. 'This—is just a private matter, and nothin' to do with—with anythin' much.'

But at last she agreed, if Toby would step out of the room with her, to tell him. In the hall, in a half-whisper, she began: ' 'Tis this way. Mrs Langman has got nine children. Her's not an old woman neither, not more'n thirty-two. Well, when her was over at The Laurels Mrs Milne comes into the kitchen and sees her, and says: "Good afternoon, Mrs Langman," says Mrs Milne, "how are you and how's the family?" "Oh, Mrs Milne, ma'am," says Lucy Langman, "I'm expectin' again."

Mrs Milne, 'er looks sympathetic and says: "Dear, dear," 'er says, "that must be a blow to you." " 'Tis that indeed," says Lucy Langman, "I don't know what us'll do with eleven mouths to feed already—and then," 'er says, "when's it goin' to stop? How many more am I goin' to have? Because," 'er says, "you know what men are." Mrs Milne don't say if she do or she don't, 'er just says: "But, my dear Mrs Langman, you can stop it whenever you want." Lucy Langman shakes her head and says as Mrs Milne don't know Langman. "Why," says Mrs Milne, laughin', "I don't mean that. But you can go to the clinic in Wallaford, where there's a very nice lady doctor, and I'll pay your fare into Wallaford, and the consultation's free, so it won't cost you anything, and you needn't have any more children." Lucy Langman just sits there starin' at her, but Martha lets out a scream. "Birth-control!" her cries. " 'Tis a deadly sin!" Mrs Milne says no, 'tis not, and Martha says as it says so in the Bible."

Mrs Eggbear drew a long breath. Once she had got into her story she had enjoyed telling it. 'You must forgive me tellin' you a story like that, Mr Dyke,' she went on, 'like women mostly only tell amongst themselves, but you asked for it. And the long and the short of it is, you see, that Martha believes Mrs Milne is a tool of the Evil One, sent to snare her poor sister, and Lucy's so scared o' Martha she dursen't do anythin'. Myself,' said Mrs Eggbear, 'I'm tolerant. I'd have liked to have a big family myself, and haven't had none. But nine and expectin' another . . .' She shook her head musingly.

'Thanks, Mrs Eggbear,' said Toby, 'I'm very grateful to you. It isn't quite the story I was expecting. Seems to me to show Mrs Milne in a not unfavourable light, though she wasn't, perhaps, particularly perceptive. Thanks very much, though. Now let's go back to your husband. I've got something to show him.'

Strange expressions chased one another over Eggbear's face as he read the cable.

Toby explained.

Eggbear's eyes grew absent-minded. He chewed at his lip.

Toby brought out the Maxwell letters. 'And I've reason for believing,' he said, 'that the missing suitcase will be found at The Laurels. George and I, we worked it out.'

'How?' said Eggbear.

So Toby explained that too. He left it, however, as a theory; he omitted the verification.

Eggbear stuffed tobacco into his pipe with heavy, deliberate fingers. While Toby was speaking he nodded from time to time, but his gaze still had that inward look.

'Yes,' he said, 'I get it.' He sighed. 'But maybe—' He stopped himself, and at last his meditative glance sought Toby's. 'Maybe I belong not to say murder yet awhile. Maybe 'tis over hasty like. Maybe 'tis jumpin' to conclusions.'

'I'm beginning to get tired of the look of this house,' said George the next morning, as once more he, Toby and Eggbear approached The Laurels. 'I find myself wishing each time I come face to face with it that maybe it'll have turned green in the night. Say, Tobe, when are we going to London?'

'Won't be long now,' said Toby, 'that's to say, I don't *think* it'll be long now.'

'You don't think. You don't think of me pining for the smell of a back-street. You don't think of anything but your own pleasures—crime and low company. You don't think . . .'

His muttering was interrupted by Eggbear. 'This afternoon Inspector Whitear in to Wallaford, he'll be along.'

'Oh,' said Toby, 'they're beginning to sit up and take notice, are they?'

'That's right,' said Eggbear. 'Reckon he'd like a talk with you.'

Toby nodded. 'What sort of man?' he asked.

'Always has luck with sweepstakes,' said Eggbear, 'and his tip on a dog's worth havin'. Mornin', Ruby,' he went on, as, in answer to his ring, the front door was opened, 'missus in?'

Ruby nodded, but would not let them in until she had Mrs Milne's word that she was willing to see them. But while they were being kept waiting the door of the drawing-room was suddenly opened and Daphne looked out.

'I thought it was you—' But seeing Eggbear beside Toby she stopped and looked as if she wished she had not shown herself to them. 'You—d'you mind if—I think you'd better come in here,' she floundered. Her cheeks had flamed under their light dusting of rouge. 'Isn't it t-t-terrible how cold it is? It just goes on and on, doesn't it? I don't like the cold, do you, Sergeant Eggbear? Though it's good for the land, isn't it? I mean, it kills pests or something, doesn't it? But I—I—'

But noticing the amusement on Toby's face, she fell silent.

Eggbear smiled at her paternally, George, prowling round the room, picked up a magazine from a chair and began to flutter its pages, Toby crossed to a window and looked out at a lawn that was crusted with the moonstone shimmer of hoar-frost. Yet Daphne's fingers went on plucking at the neck of her dress; her blue eyes, dwelling on the sleek, dark head outlined against the window, were full of nervous misery.

From somewhere out in the quiet countryside a noise reached them, a vibrant clatter. George looked up from his paper.

'Boy-friend arriving,' he remarked.

Daphne's mouth worked. But before her sudden movement towards the door could take her out, Toby swung round.

'Please stay!' Then, as if realizing how sharply he had rapped it out: 'D'you mind?' And he smiled, at his most charming.

Daphne dropped limply into a chair.

In the hall, a quick, decisive tread sounded on the polished boards. At the same time, out on the roads, the rattle of Adrian's three-wheeler came nearer. Mrs Milne entered, nodded briefly to the three of them, and sat down. Her attention was on Toby, yet she spoke to Sergeant Eggbear.

'More letters,' she asked, 'or is it perhaps the driver of that sports car?'

'No, ma'am,' he said, ' 'tis the corpse.'

'I thought,' she said, 'that he was dead and buried.'

'Yes, ma'am, and identified—so us thought.'

'So you—' She turned swiftly to Toby. 'Would you mind telling me? West Country narration's very slow.'

'But sure, very sure,' said Toby. 'This is the sergeant's night out. You listen to him.'

Her eyes flamed dangerously. 'Well, sergeant?'

'Have you ever heard, ma'am,' said Eggbear heavily, 'of Henry Rhymer?'

'No,' she said.

'You'm quite certain o' that?'

'Eggbear,' she said, 'you're an excellent man, but it's a pity one has to tell you everything twice. I have never heard of Henry Rhymer—only of Thomas.'

'Eh?' said Eggbear. 'Thomas?' His brow furrowed, and he looked at Toby for a lead.

'True Thomas,' Toby explained, 'who was abducted by the queen of Elfland. No concern of ours, Sammy—I don't think they ever found the body.'

'Oh,' said Eggbear. 'Now, ma'am, you'm quite certain in your mind—'

'Yes,' she said wearily.

'—quite certain that the name of Henry Rhymer is totally unfamiliar to you?'

'Yes!'

'And,' said Toby, 'she isn't even interested. Hasn't even asked: "Why Henry Rhymer all of a sudden?" '

'Sometimes,' she answered him, 'I can think as quickly as you, Mr Dyke. You've hinted at a misidentification of the dead man. Presumably, then, the man we thought was Shelley Maxwell has somehow been identified as this Henry Rhymer. Well, I'm relieved to hear it. I'd sooner not be responsible for the death of my neighbours' only son. Apart from that . . .' She made a gesture of indifference.

Toby came across the room and sat down on a chair near her. Just as he began to speak the door opened quietly and Adrian came in. He went to Daphne's side and sat on the arm of her chair, nodding to the others without interrupting them.

'Listen,' said Toby, 'Shelley Maxwell died last May. He died in South Africa, in hospital, from appendicitis. He had a friend called Henry Rhymer. Henry Rhymer informed the authorities that, so far as he knew, Maxwell had no relatives. He saw to his funeral and took over his belongings—including an old leather suitcase. Did you say something, Miss Milne?'

'Me?' said Daphne. 'No, I—didn't, I was just fidgeting.'

Toby went on: 'He also took over Shelley Maxwell's identity. He knew all his affairs, you see, and all about his family. He knew that Maxwell got letters from his mother, and that those letters contained money. So he set himself to learn Maxwell's handwriting. But either forgery wasn't one of his natural talents and came rather slowly, or else he was badly pressed for cash and didn't want to waste time. He wrote a letter with his left hand, saying he'd hurt his right. It worked splendidly. Lady Maxwell not only swallowed it, but sent an extra large remittance to cover possible doctor's bills. He wrote another letter or so with his left hand, then, when he felt sure he'd got the forgery good enough, went over to the right, and kept that up until about two months ago. Then he wrote another letter with his left hand. One can assume he was trying it on to see whether he could get some extra money again. He did, and bought a passage to England. We don't know why he wanted to come to England. Perhaps he'd got something on Shelley Maxwell, and thought the parents might pay to have it kept quiet. By revealing himself to the Maxwells he was giving up a small but steady income, so he must have felt sure he'd got on to something a good deal bigger. But perhaps it wasn't the Maxwells he was after at all. Perhaps it was someone else.'

'Meaning me,' said Mrs Milne.

'Yes,' said Toby, 'that's just what I was coming to.'

She sat staring straight before her.

Adrian murmured: 'Some sleuth! However did you find it all out, Dyke?'

Her eyes still on the wall opposite, in a voice even harsher than usual, she said: 'I thought your job was to find out who's been writing those anonymous letters.'

'Oh, I'm still trying to catch up with him,' said Toby. 'When I know as much as he does, I dare say I'll be able to point at him.'

'Him?' said Adrian. 'Don't women ever take to that form of making trouble?'

'Him or her,' said Toby.

With a little note-book open on his knee and a pencil pointing at an entry in it, Eggbear observed: 'But all the same, you was expectin' somebody Tuesday evenin', eh, Mrs Milne?'

Her head moved abruptly as she turned to him. 'I was—?'

'Yes, ma'am, expectin' a man about half-past six Tuesday evenin', before you set out for the badminton.'

'What's this?' said Toby. 'Sammy, you never told me anything about that. George, what d'you think of that, Sammy's been holding out on us.'

Eggbear went on stolidly: 'Constable Leat, in conversation with Ruby Leat on Sunday afternoon, learnt as you'd been expectin' a man to visit you, because Ruby overheard you to say—ahem—"He's late." Then at six-forty-five approx. you said as you couldn't wait, and went out to the car. Perhaps, ma'am—' and he looked up from his note-book—'you'd care to call Ruby in and question her.'

Mrs Milne shook her head. 'Oh no, it's perfectly true. Only it hasn't anything to do with all this. Perhaps I should have told you sooner, because, of course, I can see how it must strike you. It just never occurred to me. You see, the man I was expecting was Mr Laws.'

With obvious surprise Daphne looked up at him as he sat on the arm of her chair. There was an odd expression on his face; his eyebrows had lifted as if he were faintly puzzled.

'Adrian?' said Daphne.

'Yes,' said her mother. 'You remember, you'd just gone off to London in a rage because of the things I'd been saying about him. I decided I'd better have a talk with him, a fairly cool and reasonable talk without you there to confuse the issue. I wrote him a note, asking him to drop in, if he could manage it, about six o'clock. But he couldn't, or didn't want to, and at a quarter to seven I decided I couldn't wait any longer on the chance that he'd turn up. That's your explanation, Eggbear. I'm sorry it's probably a disappointment.'

Eggbear made a jotting or two, and looked at Adrian.

'That right, Mr Laws? You got the note.'

The young man was pushing his fingers through his tawny hair. 'Yes, of course—that is, I mean—oh, Anna, what's the good of it? They're bound to find out.'

She regarded him blankly. 'Find out what?'

His face showed distress and bewilderment. 'I'd back you up all I could if I could see the slightest good in it. But, well, it'd be so easy to prove that—you see, I'm never up very early in the morning, and my charwoman always takes in the post. She knows absolutely everything about my correspondence. So if anyone went and questioned her—I mean—damn it, I'm most frightfully sorry, Anna, but it just isn't any good.'

She was leaning forward tensely in her chair. 'You mean you never got that note?'

'Of course, it may have gone missing in the post,' he said hurriedly. 'I dare say it did. It does happen sometimes.'

She repeated: 'You never got that note!'

He shook his head regretfully.

Anna Milne rose suddenly to her feet and turned away.

Daphne exclaimed: 'Adrian, I do think you might have—!'

He slipped an arm round her shoulders. 'Absolutely no good, my dear. Wouldn't have paid in the end. Don't be angry with me. But I don't think I'll stay. Not the right moment for making peaceful approaches, d'you think? I'll go and drive round and round for a bit in my little car. Coming with me?'

She shook her head, her eyes on her mother. Adrian shrugged, nodded to the men, and went out. Mrs Milne turned round.

'So,' she said, looking at Eggbear, 'my story's no good.'

'Well, ma'am—' he began uneasily.

She laughed—an unattractive sound.

Toby remarked: 'Perhaps you'd like to alter it.'

'Oddly enough, not,' she answered.

'Perhaps you're wise,' he said.

'After all,' she said, 'it isn't a bad story. I rather like it. It's simple, it's homely, it's easy to repeat. The next one might be even less reliable. Now is there anything else you want to ask me? I'm not sure, Eggbear, that you oughtn't to have warned me that anything I say may be taken down and used in evidence. And next time you come I'm not sure I shan't have a solicitor present.'

'Certainly, ma'am, if you wish,' he answered without expression.

Outside in the car on the way back to Chovey, the sergeant said: 'Her'd have to be put through a mangle to squeeze any admissions out o' she. I'll lay she knows all about this Henry Rhymer. That story o' hers!'

'Yes,' said Toby, 'and it's queer she trusted Laws to back her up when there's so little friendship between them. What I'd like is a chance to talk to the girl. She wants to talk to me, but she's afraid of something.'

'Tobe always thinks any nice girl wants to talk to him only she's afraid,' George explained to the sergeant.

'No,' said Toby, 'there's something really queer—'

But George interrupted: 'Queer! I'll give you something queer to think about. When that bloke Laws up and contradicts her and she turns away all champing with anger to the window . . .'

'Well?' said Toby.

'Well,' said George, 'why, *why*, I ask you, was she looking as pleased as hell? Why—and maybe since you're a brilliant and intelligent bloke you can tell me—why was it that when her story'd just had a hole blown in it big enough to swallow a horse and cart, why should she pick on that particular moment to start grinning all over her face?'

Inspector Whitear had chiselled features, a delicate

golden tan, violet eyes and a streak of a moustache like a plucked eyebrow on his upper lip.

He was intelligent, fairly well educated, and naturally friendly. Only a high-pitched, wheezy voice detracted from an arresting personality.

'Now here's something you'll be interested in,' he told Eggbear and Toby. 'Information just came in before I started out. That suitcase—'

Eggbear interrupted with a slight cough. 'In my report—'

'Ah yes, you've located it, I know. Good work. Very good work. But nevertheless, here's a point of interest. We've been making inquiries around the place about that suitcase, and this morning the cloakroom attendant at Knightsteignton—'

'Knightsteignton?' said Toby.

'Station before Wallaford,' Whitear replied. 'This cloakroom attendant gets to hear of it and does a bit of thinking, and then phones up to tell us that on Thursday morning a lady came and collected a suitcase that answered to the description of the one we were looking for—an old, battered, leather suitcase. What's more, it had the initials SM stamped on it. She was a young lady, smartly dressed; he didn't remember much else about her. Then on the evening of the same day another lady comes in. He remembered her a bit better—middle-aged, dark, expensive fur coat, diamond rings—'

'Mrs Milne,' said Eggbear.

'Yes, and Daphne in the morning,' said Toby. 'I knew that girl came in somewhere.'

'Quite, quite,' said Whitear. 'Well, this lady in the fur coat comes in and asks him does he remember who it was that deposited the suitcase and when. He says yes he does, it was Wednesday midday, and the person who did it was—'

'A tall, dark man with glasses,' chanted George from his place very close to the stove.

'That's right,' said Whitear, looking round at him and nodding. 'That's right, a tall, dark—excuse me, Mr er—?'

'Pilskin,' said George.

'—Mr Pilskin, but haven't I seen you somewhere before?'

Shaking his head emphatically, George sank closer to the stove.

Whitear continued: 'A tall, dark man with glasses. It appears, in fact, that this man picked the suitcase up in Wallaford and went straight off and deposited it in Knightsteignton.'

'I'll bet,' said Toby, 'that—'

'How much?' said Whitear quickly.

'Any amount you like,' said Toby, 'that he found time to open it on the way. You know, Sam, this turns things round a bit. We've been rather assuming that the man who collected the suitcase was doing it *for* Mrs Milne. But now, unless she was trying to cover his tracks—'

'Which she'd be quite spry enough for, you take my word,' said Eggbear.

Toby nodded. 'Yes, but if by any chance the inquiry was a genuine one, then it's between the man and Daphne that we've got to look for collaboration.' He picked up one of the pencils lying on Eggbear's desk and began to tap with it.

'Well,' said Eggbear, 'that makes it easier to understand. I've always had a feeling that man'd turn out to be young Laws, only I couldn't see him and Mrs Milne carryin' out a job o' work in harmony like. But if 'tis Miss Daphne then there ain't no difficulty.'

'Except . . .' said Toby, frowning and still tapping away with the pencil. Suddenly he glanced up. 'Hullo, George,' he said, 'where you off to?'

'Phone my girl,' said George and went out. Toby, the pencil growing still in his fingers, looked after him with a smile.

Whitear waited a moment, then prompted him: 'You don't think the daughter's mixed up in it, Mr Dyke?'

'Oh, I'm sure she is,' said Toby. 'No doubt about it at all. Only so's a retired major who can't sleep at nights, and hates his brother; and so, perhaps, is the brother, and perhaps even the brother's wife. And when, I wonder, is the next helpful hint from the anonymous letterwriter coming? I'm sure he won't leave us in the lurch at this point. I think, if you don't mind, I'm going to pop over to the pub to see if there's any afternoon post for me.'

But when he was out in the street Toby did not go towards the Ring of Bells, but, sauntering in the opposite direction, stopped and waited outside the post office—or grocer's, or tobacconist's, or chemist's, as one might choose to call it. After a few minutes George came out.

Lighting a cigarette, Toby inquired: 'Did you have the idea I think you did, George?'

'My idea,' said George, 'was train or car.'

'That's right,' said Toby. 'Which was it?'

'Well, I've been talking to the cloakroom fellow,' said George, 'but when it comes to the local dialect I find I'm just an amateur with the telephone. Still, I gather he's certain the man arrived by train. There's an eleven forty-seven from Wallaford that gets to Knightsteignton at twelve-three. He says the man came by that. Swears to it.'

'And,' said Toby, 'as you've probably remembered, Major Maxwell's car was out of order.'

From behind a voice broke in upon them: 'Mr Dyke, sir.'

'Hullo,' said Toby.

It was the postman.

'I got a letter for 'e, Mr Dyke,' he said. 'Shall I give'n to 'e now or go on and leave'n for 'e up to the hotel?'

'Glad to have it now,' said Toby, and, taking it, tore it open.

'RIVERFIELD HANTS NOVEMBER 1917,' said the anonymous correspondent.

CHAPTER 12

In the morning twilight, some time before half-past seven and eight o'clock, Toby stirred in bed and groaned miserably.

With eyes that detested the sight of day, he blinked, and saw a jar of barley-sugar standing on the corner of the washstand.

The washstand was just within his reach.

Ten minutes later George came in and found Toby, his cheek bulging, lying with hands folded under his head, his gaze following the interweavings of the roses on the wallpaper opposite with a look of almost human interest.

George shut the door, sat down on a corner of the bed, and reached for Toby's cigarettes.

Sucking, Toby remarked: 'You know, it works.'

'Didn't I tell you?' said George.

'Mmm.' The bulge shifted from one cheek to the other. 'George, I've been thinking.'

A match spurted in the half-light as George lit the cigarette.

'How d'you feel,' said Toby, 'about another little job of housebreaking?'

'Well, Tobe, I'm not in the best of practice, and then there's the question of conscience, and—'

'I want that flask, George.'

'That flask! But that ain't housebreaking, that's only in the garage. Oh, I could get that for you—goes without saying.'

'Then get it, will you, as soon as you can? And don't handle it.'

George nodded.

'And tell me something,' said Toby. 'This letter—' He reached for his jacket and extracted the sheet of paper from a pocket. 'Anything special strike you about it?'

George stared at it for a minute or two. 'That "NOVEMBER",' he said, 'it's in a funny sort of type.'

'Yes, that's true. Not the sort of type you often see in newspapers, is it? But doesn't anything else strike you? . . . Oh, well, it's only a guess at this stage, but d'you know, George, I've an idea this fellow's played right into our hands. Now see about that flask—and remember, don't handle it!'

Later in the morning Toby said to Sergeant Eggbear: 'Sammy, I think it'd be a good idea to find out what Stuart Maxwell was doing with himself all Wednesday morning.'

'Wednesday,' said Eggbear, 'why, what was Wednesday, Toby?'

'Wednesday was the day the suitcase was picked up from the Wallaford Left-Luggage and taken to Knightsteignton.'

'Ah,' said Eggbear, 'so 'twas.' He nursed his round red chin in his hand. 'So 'twas. So you'm a-thinkin' . . .'

'I'm going to find out myself what Laws was doing,' said Toby. 'I'm going out there now. Where's his place? How do I get to it?'

''Tis up over the other side o' Purbrook,' said Eggbear, 'right on the edge of the moor. You keep straight on when you get through Purbrook till the road splits in two, then you go to the right, and the cottage is about half a mile down—a sort o' stone place, lonesome, you might say, only these authors, I allow, they like it that way. But I was goin' to tell you, Toby, last night Whitear spent a long time talkin' to some folks in Riverfield on the telephone. He talked to the police station and the vicarage and the doctor.'

'Did he get anything?'

'Not much. But he's put the police there on to askin' questions.'

'I see. Well, I'm on my way to visit friend Laws. And you'll deal with the major?'

'That's right,' said Eggbear.

Toby mounted into his stately car and drove away.

Of the two roads to Purbrook he took the one he knew. Down its narrow length, round its sudden blind corners, over its humpbacked bridges, the big, old car with its seventeen-year-old brakes made necessarily a slow and cautious progress. But it reached Purbrook at last, threaded its way through the one or two streets that composed the village, and continued along a road that divided in two a stretch of heathery common. Straight ahead lay Dartmoor, hunching its round shoulders, always a little sinister in its bleakness.

Adrian's cottage was easy to find. There were no others near it. Of grey stone, with its shabby thatch repaired in places with sheets of corrugated iron, its garden a neglected patch of sprouted cabbage-stalks, its fence broken down, there was little about it to fit the mind's usual picture of a country cottage. Behind it the ground rose in a steep slope, grown over by rusty heather and bracken beaten to the earth by wind and rain.

At Toby's knocking the door was opened by an elderly woman in a hat and a print overall.

'No,' she replied to his question, 'Mr Laws is in to Purbrook, doin' his shoppin'. Is he expectin' you?'

'Not particularly,' said Toby, 'but if you think he won't be long I'd like to wait.'

'We-ell, maybe he won't be long,' she said doubtfully, 'but with he you never can say for certain. Maybe he'll be straight back, and then again maybe he'll think of visitin' someone, or maybe that little car of his will break down and he won't be back till afternoon. But if you'd like to come in and wait . . .' She shrugged her shoulders.

'I'll wait for a bit, anyway,' said Toby.

She made no objection, and allowed him through the kitchen into a small sitting-room beyond it. She apologized for the fact that she would have to be in and out of the room, because she was doing the upstairs and this was the only way to get at the staircase.

'But make yourself comfortable,' she said, and, opening what Toby had taken to be the door of a cupboard, disappeared up the narrow stairs inside. Toby looked round him.

The room was quite pleasant though very small. It was cleanly kept and as tidy as a good charwoman, struggling with a man of more or less literary habits, could make it. Probably when Adrian had first come there he had lavished love and thought upon the little room, giving the walls their coating of light green, choosing the russet for the curtains and the covering of the one armchair. A Gauguin reproduction hung above the fireplace, bookshelves filled the recesses to right and left, an odd piece of sculpture like half of a man's head parted from the other half by an explosion, stood on the mantelpiece. There was matting on the floor, and a bowl of slightly faded chrysanthemums on the table. Also there was a telephone.

Surprise showed on Toby's face when he noticed the telephone. He sat down on the arm of the chair and stared at it. It stood on the corner of a battered but probably once beautiful walnut bureau. Toby frowned at the telephone. A slight, hissing sound came through his teeth. Then he stood up again and started looking over the bookshelves.

The heavy steps of the charwoman sounded on the stairs just then, and she emerged through the door, carrying a tin of floor-polish and a mop. Toby turned round.

'Lonely spot out here,' he said.

'Yes, 'tis lonely,' she agreed, 'but I don't have far to come. I come across the fields, don't even have to take my overall off, 'cause I come across the fields. Peter Saunders don't mind. I said to he when he saw me: "I'm just goin' up over to do for Mr Laws," I said, "goin' across your fields, Mr Saunders." "That's all right, Mrs Rice," he says. So that's how 'tis, ye see—I come across the fields.'

'Yes, I see,' said Toby, 'you come across the fields.'

She nodded. 'In me overall,' she said, and went on into the kitchen.

On her return journey Toby started again. 'Don't expect you get many posts out here, do you?'

'Twice a day,' she said, 'same as most places. But if 'tis only a postcard comes by the afternoon post and the postman sees as 'tis nothin' important, he don't bring'n till morning.'

'Ah,' said Toby, 'but you *do* get an afternoon post?'

'Yes, and they say us'll get the electricity in another year or so. Us signed a petition for'n last year.'

'But it comes—the post, I mean—after you've gone home, I expect, doesn't it?'

'Oh yes, it don't come till five, and I'm never home later than three. I just get Mr Laws' dinner and wash up, and then I go home. I go home across the fields, you see, so I wouldn't want to wait till dark.'

'Yes, I see, I see. I see—a certain amount.' He added: 'But not much. It's murky.' He turned again to the bookcase, while Mrs Rice, with her dusters, went upstairs.

He had already run his eye over the titles of most of the books. Now he began rummaging on a shelf which was filled, not with books, but with periodicals. They were jammed in, some upright, some on their sides, completely filling the space between that shelf and the next. Probably it was Mrs Rice who had taken to shoving them in there when she found them on the floor. Toby pulled out one or two and glanced through them.

He had one of them open in his hands when the noise made by Adrian's three-wheeler reached him from the road outside. He replaced the paper, then pulled it out again, and was standing on the hearth-rug, reading it, when Adrian came in.

Adrian's face looked nipped by cold, his hair was windblown. The Sunbeam outside had warned him of Toby's presence, and he was smiling. But the smile was ironic, not friendly.

'Hullo, Dyke, sleuthing?' He pushed the armchair close to the fire and sat down. 'Damn cold. Rotten in an open car, but at any rate the old woman's kept the fire up. What can I do for you, or is this pure friendship?'

Toby turned over a page.

'Quite interesting, this,' he remarked. 'I haven't run across it before.'

'That? Oh, it's not much good,' said Adrian. 'I don't often buy it. But they took a story of mine. Is that the number?' He looked to see which number it was that Toby was examining. 'No, that's the October. It was in the next. They don't pay one, of course; the thing's an utter failure commercially. But just now and then it does publish something quite passable. It's not really much good, though—nothing like it might be.'

'I'd like to see the one with your story in it,' said Toby.

Adrian gave his ironic smile, but he reached out towards the shelf and started a search amongst the papers there for the November number of the small monthly they were discussing. It was called *New Voices*. Short stories, poems, two or three pages of politics, some book and play reviews, made it the same as most literary monthlies, only its preciousness was unusually blatant. It was printed in a curious, defiant-looking type, with an irregular right-hand margin, its cover had an all-over design of green on white, a pattern of cockle shells, and the pages were bound together with a spiral spring.

After searching for a moment, Adrian let his hand drop. 'No, I don't know where it's got to,' he said. 'I expect Mrs Rice has put it somewhere. What is it you want, Dyke, apart from a chance to pull my work to pieces?'

Toby turned sideways, leaning an elbow on the mantelpiece. He looked down at Adrian.

'Where were you a week ago this morning?'

The question startled Adrian. He at once looked defensive. He leant back in the chair, folding his hands behind his tawny head.

'A week ago . . . last Wednesday morning? The moment you ask me my mind goes absolutely blank. Can't you remind me of something else that happened then? Perhaps it'll make me remember.'

'It was the morning after Mrs Milne had her accident.'

'Ah, of course.' He frowned. 'Wednesday . . .'

'The morning after the badminton game in Purbrook,' Toby prompted. 'Were you there, by the way?'

'Good Lord, no. I joined the club when I first came here, for the amusement of the thing, but once I'd soaked up the atmosphere of local gossip, I couldn't stand it. For gossip give me a pub, not a genteel collection of women with their knitting, and retired majors and colonels. Even Anna Milne used to take her knitting there.'

'Wednesday,' said Toby.

A faint smile crossed Adrian's face. 'All right, I'll get there in time.'

'On Wednesday *evening*,' said Toby, 'you dined at Chovey Place, in company with Mrs Milne and Major Maxwell. After it the three of you came into the Ring of Bells for a drink. That was the first time we met. Does that help at all to remind you what you did in the morning?'

'It does,' said Adrian immediately, 'I've just remembered the whole thing. On Wednesday morning I went for a walk.'

'Alone?'

'Yes.'

'Anyone see you?'

'I shouldn't think so. I walked across the moor. Took a couple of sandwiches in my pocket, and didn't get back till the afternoon. I'm afraid'—and he smiled again more openly—'that isn't the sort of answer you were wanting.'

'I could have done with something a bit tidier,' Toby admitted.

'Something easier to corroborate or easier to disprove—I know. But that's the way things happen. But why does it matter where I was on Wednesday morning? What was going on then that disturbed your sense of the fair and square, the normal and insignificant?'

Toby was looking down into the fire. With one hand at his mouth he tugged at his lower lip. Suddenly he looked up.

'May I use your telephone?'

'Go ahead,' said Adrian.

'What's Mrs Milne's number?'

'Chovey 79.'

'Thanks,' said Toby, and picked up the instrument from its corner of the walnut bureau.

While he was giving the number and waiting, he was watched by Adrian with a steady gaze in which wariness and curiosity were quite unconcealed. As Toby began to speak, Adrian lit a cigarette, but his eyes did not leave Toby's face. The firelight lit little tongues of flame on his spectacles.

'Can I speak to Mrs Milne?' said Toby.

During the pause that followed he heard Adrian begin to hum very softly under his breath.

A click in the receiver and a voice said in Toby's ear: 'Mrs Milne speaking.'

Toby grinned at Adrian. 'I've only just learnt,' he said, 'that Adrian Laws has a telephone.'

She answered: 'Why do I need to know that?'

'But you know that he has one?'

'Of course,' she said.

Adrian blew a thin stream of smoke before him.

Toby went on: 'When you wanted him to come and see you, why did you write to him? I mean the time when your daughter was in London, and you wanted to discuss her with him. Why didn't you ring him up?'

'Because when I first thought of it I didn't think of asking him to come and see me. I went to see him. But he wasn't in. So I scribbled a note and pushed it under the door, saying I'd be in that evening until half-past six.'

'A note,' said Toby, 'yes, that's the word that stuck in my mind. You said "note" each time, and he replied as if you'd said "letter".'

'He replied,' she said, 'as he, for some reason, saw fit.'

'Yet it gave you considerable pleasure.'

There was silence.

'Isn't that so?' said Toby.

'I'm sorry,' she said. 'I can't hear you.'

'His reply,' said Toby, '—it gave you considerable pleasure.'

'There's an awful buzzing,' she said. 'Try hitting your instrument. That clears it sometimes.'

'I've no grudge against this instrument,' said Toby, 'it hasn't done me any harm. See if you can hear this. Last night I got another anonymous letter.'

In his chair by the fire Adrian stirred. His gaze on Toby was suddenly concentrated. His lips parted as if he were about to interrupt.

At her end of the wire Anna Milne said: 'Yes?'

'Whoever it is that sends them,' said Toby, 'has made a serious blunder this time.'

'Well,' she said impatiently, 'what was it, what did it say?'

'It said simply: "RIVERFIELD HANTS NOVEMBER 1917".'

There was another short silence. 'And you say,' she resumed hesitantly, 'that there's a serious blunder in that?'

'You don't see it?' said Toby. 'Think it over. You're good at spotting the implications of this fellow's style. And goodbye for the present—I'm neglecting my host.' He hung up the receiver before she could say any more.

Adrian was regarding him very strangely. His look was positively shrinking.

'D'you know, you're a cruel devil, Dyke,' he murmured in his soft voice. 'You've got a cat-and-mouse mind.'

'So has someone else around the place,' said Toby, coming to stand on the hearthrug close above the young man. 'And returning to the affair of the note, what about it?'

'Well, what about it?' said Adrian. 'I don't understand.'

'Yesterday morning,' said Toby, 'Mrs Milne made the statement that the man she had been expecting on the Tuesday evening was you. She said she'd written a note, asking you to come and see her. Now either she was telling the truth or she wasn't—'

'Logic,' said Adrian.

'Yes. Well, if she was telling the truth, you weren't.'

Adrian nodded.

'If she *wasn't* telling the truth,' Toby went on, 'she was relying on you to back her up. You didn't.'

Adrian nodded again.

'You said,' said Toby, 'that the fact that she'd never written to you could too easily be traced for the story to be any good. Your charwoman, you said, handles all your post. But Mrs Milne says that she never wrote to you by post. I'd wondered why she should have as soon as I saw you'd a telephone. She says she came out to see you, didn't find you, and pushed a note under the door. But even if that weren't true, your Mrs Rice informs me that you get an afternoon post here about five o'clock, but that she never stays later than three. No, Laws, even if Mrs Milne's story isn't any good, yours isn't either. You could easily have backed her up without being caught out. Your reason for not backing up your Daphne's mother was one that you didn't divulge. So, as I said, what about it?'

Adrian's lips had closed into a hard line. He gave no answer for a while. At length he said: 'All right, I'll tell you why I didn't back up her story. I hate that woman. I loathe her from the bottom of my soul. Is that good enough?'

'Yes,' said Toby, 'always supposing that what she said about your being expected wasn't true. Though,' he added thoughtfully, 'even if it was true, the same answer might reasonably cover it.'

'I hate her,' said Adrian, 'as I've never hated anyone in my life. It isn't only for the way she dominates Daphne, tries to keep the poor girl a child and break her of any hopes of developing a mind or a will of her own—though, my God, if you could watch her brooding over her young it'd sicken you all right!—and it isn't for her endless little sneers at me, or the way she's got her claws into my poor cousin Stuart. But she's a fundamentally coarse-grained creature. She's cheap to the very core. She's vulgar, rotten—she's one of those things that leaves a smear behind them. She's—' He stopped himself. His voice had not risen above its usual soft note, but it was vicious as the biting of acid.

Toby said: 'I see,' and waited.

When Adrian said nothing more, but only started chewing at his thumbnail, Toby added: 'And what d'you think happened at Riverfield, Hants, in November, 1917?'

Adrian started, withdrawing his gaze, as if with difficulty, from the fire. But he only shrugged his shoulders.

'Odd,' said Toby, 'that the writer should make a mistake like that.'

'I don't understand,' said Adrian wearily, 'I'm afraid I don't think quickly enough for you. There's been another letter . . . Is there anything else you want to know?'

This time Toby shook his head, and, to the plain satisfaction of Adrian, took his departure.

But if there was nothing further that Toby wanted to know, or thought he could obtain, from Adrian, it was quickly apparent that there was something he wanted to know which he believed might be told by Adrian's ash-bin.

He drove his car only a short way down the road, then left it and walked back. The window of the sitting-room looked out towards the moor and away from the road, so that it was easy for him to reach the door of the cottage without being noticed. Had Adrian emerged, Toby could probably have thought of some new question to ask. But no one saw him, and he was able to reach the ash-bin, which stood some way to the right of the kitchen door, without difficulty.

Yet though he had taken the trouble to come back, his search in the ash-bin for what he thought might be there was perfunctory. He had picked up a stick, and with this he prodded about in the top layer of ashes. It was mostly wood-ash, feathery and light, lifting in a fine dust as he stirred it. Almost at once a piece of wire was revealed. It was coiled like a slack spring, about nine inches long.

With a look of surprise on his face, as if this were positively too easy, Toby pocketed it, and, walking quickly, returned to his car.

CHAPTER 13

In Chovey, Toby drove straight down the street to the police station. But another car, a small blue saloon, was just pulling up before it. As Toby stopped his behind this car, he saw Major Maxwell get out. The major stood hesitantly on the pavement for a moment, then he caught sight of Toby and came quickly towards him.

'Dyke, I'm glad to have found you. I called at your pub, but they said you'd gone out. So I made up my mind to go to the police. That's to say—yes, I'd made up my mind, I was just going in. But if I could have a word with you . . . I mean, I'm not sure that there's really any point in bothering the police with this, but it's on my mind, worrying me a good deal, as a matter of fact, and—'

'All right,' said Toby, 'we'll go back to the pub. Don't happen to have seen George, do you?'

'No,' said the major, walking beside the car as Toby began to back along the street, 'no, I don't think so, though if I had I dare say I shouldn't have noticed. I've been thoroughly upset. I'm run down, you know—got shockingly out of condition. I must have a change, I think, a cruise or something, get out of this damn climate, go to Malta or somewhere like that. Ever been to Malta? Wonderful climate.' He talked on unceasingly until Toby had parked the car and taken him into the empty coffee-room of the Ring of Bells.

But even then he roved about, started irrelevant subjects, dropped them and started others. His hands, as he filled his pipe, were quivering. Suddenly he held one of them up in front of Toby.

'Look at that. Can't keep it steady. That's the state I'm in. I need a tonic—or a change. Yes, I'll go for a cruise, I think. Some sea air and a nice, jolly atmosphere. Can't bear jolly atmospheres usually, but it does you good now and then to be taken out of yourself. I'll go for a cruise.'

'Since I'm not a doctor, a nerve specialist or a travel agent,' said Toby, 'why did you want to see me?'

The major drew a chair close to him and spoke in a low voice. 'I'll tell you. Someone's taken my revolver.'

'Your—?'

'My revolver. My old service revolver. Sometime this morning.'

In the early dusk already beginning to darken in the coffee-room, Toby observed Major Maxwell carefully. But he was certainly sober.

'How d'you know it was this morning?' said Toby.

'I do know. It's only by chance I know, but as it happens I was looking at it last night. I put it back in its case at the back of the second left-hand drawer of my desk about one o'clock last night. And now it's gone.'

'And the case?'

'No, the case is still there.'

'Closed?'

'Yes, closed.'

'Then what made you look again this morning to see if the revolver was still in it?'

The major ran one of his quivering hands over his grizzled hair.

'I think I'll tell you the truth, Dyke. I've looked at that revolver quite a number of times during the last few days. Don't mistake me, one can look at a revolver without actually—I mean, because there's an idea in one's head, it doesn't follow that there's anything concrete about it. Because I want to look at a revolver, it doesn't follow that I actually intend to kill myself. But when there's an idea in one's head and it keeps coming back, when it sometimes almost makes one believe that one is serious about it, well, getting out a revolver, you know, and handling it

—it sort of steadies you, you know, makes you realize what a long way from reality your thoughts are. As I was saying, I was looking at it last night, then I went up to bed and I'd a rotten night, rotten, and then Eggbear came out and asked me a lot of questions about where I'd been some time or other, and I didn't seem to give him the answers he wanted, and I got thoroughly jumpy, so I thought I'd drive into Wallaford and pick up some seed-catalogues. Early to be worrying about that, I know, still, I like to have them to look at. Then I came back to lunch at The Laurels and didn't go back to the cottage until about an hour ago. And the revolver was gone. I sat down at my desk, and pulled open the drawer, and took out the case, and—it was gone. Gone, Dyke! Stolen! D'you understand what it means? D'you realize—? Oh, my God, this is hell! You've got to do something about it—d'you understand, Dyke?'

'It sounds to me,' said Toby slowly, 'as if someone didn't realize the soothing effects of a revolver on a possible suicide, and removed it for your safety. Who knew it was there?'

'Lots of people. But no, that isn't why it was taken. No, no, I'm quite certain it wasn't. No one knows what I've just been telling you, so why should they think of removing it? No, I'll tell you what I believe it is, and then you've *got* to do something. I believe—' his tense fingers were clutching Toby's sleeve—'I believe it was Mrs Milne who took it!'

'Why should she do that?' said Toby.

Maxwell jumped up and stood over Toby, his clenched fists pounding the air a few inches from Toby's chest.

'Because she's afraid. Because she's terrified. Because she's being hounded to the gallows and she doesn't believe anything can save her. That's why she took it. She isn't the kind of woman who'll sit still and let things happen to her. She couldn't—it isn't the way she's made.

There's an immense courage as well as a ghastly fatalism in Anna Milne. As soon as she's certain, as soon as she's convinced that there's no hope for her, she'll—she'll—'

'But why,' said Toby, interrupting the major's choking, 'should she become convinced that there's no hope for her, unless she's committed murder?' He paused, then added quietly: 'You believe she did, don't you?'

'No!' cried Stuart Maxwell. 'No! It's the last thing on earth I'd believe. Nothing'd make me believe it—nothing! I swear it.'

'In that case,' said Toby, 'you want *us* to believe it. I repeat, why?'

'I want *you* . . .?' The major drew away from him stood upright, suddenly sat down, and burst into a shout of laughter. He laughed with a shaking of his shoulders, a heaving of his chest. It was loud, hearty laughter, but with the sawing sound of hysteria in it.

'One or the other,' said Toby. 'Take your choice.'

At that moment the door of the coffee-room opened and George put his head round it. He saw the laughing major, looked questioningly at Toby, and, at Toby's slight nod, came in.

The major collected himself.

'But listen, Dyke, you haven't told me what you're going to do about it. You've got to get it back. You understand, don't you?—it's imperative. She may do something desperate; she's that kind of person. You don't know her as I do. What are you going to do?'

Toby's gesture with his hands expressed complete ignorance. Maxwell's face lost its animation; it looked tired and frail. He got up and said: 'Ah well, think about it, there's a good chap. Don't know what to do myself.' Nodding to George, he went out. Toby leant back, stretched out his legs, and thrust his hands deep into his pockets. He whistled a note or two, then rolled his head round, regarded George and said: 'Well?'

George sat down in the chair that the major had left.

'Sorry to've been so long, Tobe. I got talking to that girl, Ruby. She's not bad.'

'The flask?'

'Gone, Tobe.'

Toby cursed, but with indifference.

'Yes, I'd a good look,' said George, 'but nothing doing. I searched the car and one or two other places, but it's been snitched. Not in the ordinary way of domestic tidiness, I may add, because I made sure of that from Ruby. She hadn't been washing it or polishing it, or anything like that.'

'Well, it was only a try-on, anyway,' said Toby. 'I dare say it wouldn't have told us anything.'

'I've got something for you, though,' said George. 'I got an idea in my head, see, while I was chatting to Ruby. I said to her, did she happen to remember the night of the accident by any chance. She said of course she did. I said to her, did she remember when Mrs Milne left the house in her car. She said yes. I said did she happen to remember any noise soon after it. She said: "Noise?" I said: "Yes, noise." She said: "What sort of noise?" So I went to the kitchen tap and turned it on, because I'd noticed, see, that when she turned that tap on just a certain amount it started to make a rattling noise as if it was going to shake the whole house down. You know the noise taps make. Well, then I took a couple of saucepan lids and started banging them together. First, Ruby looks at me as if I've gone off my nut, but then all of a sudden she gives a scream of laughter and says isn't that clever? I'm inclined to think that myself, and I keep it up, saying does she remember hearing it any time Tuesday evening. She goes on giggling for a bit, then she says come to think of it, she did, and just then Martha comes in and tells her she'll burn in hell-fire for having a man in the kitchen. But Ruby just says: "Martha, d'you remember Tuesday evening, when you said: 'There's Mr Laws arrivin' '? You did, didn't you Martha?'' And Martha says: ''Yes, I heard his car in the road. And I didn't know what he was comin' for, seein' as Miss Daphne was up to London. But he didn't come in. He just stopped a bit and drove away again.'' And then she turned me out of the kitchen with good wishes for my journey below.'

'Where we'll go together, George,' cried Toby excitedly, jumping to his feet, 'because I don't know what I'd do without you!'

In the police station later that afternoon Inspector Whitear greeted Toby and George with a flashing of his violet eyes and the friendliest of smiles. His squeaky voice was enthusiastic.

'We're getting somewhere, Mr Dyke—yes, indeed. Eh, Eggbear? We've got something, eh?'

Eggbear nodded. His face was dour. He was not responsive to Whitear's charm.

Whitear tilted his chair back at a rakish angle.

'Yes—yes, indeed. Riverfield's told us all we need to know. Nice little place, Riverfield.'

'You aren't forgetting,' said Toby, 'that somebody told you about Riverfield?'

Whitear chuckled. 'Ha, ha, we know better than that. We know our jobs, Mr Dyke. But that's a secondary matter. Poison pens are nasty things, but murder's worse.'

Toby said nothing. Whitear tilted his chair delicately backwards and forwards.

'And we've rounded up that sports car,' he observed.

'But it ain't told us nothin',' said Eggbear quickly, 'nothin' us didn't know already.'

'We-ll,' said Whitear, 'perhaps not. Perhaps—perhaps not.'

'Who was it?' said Toby.

'A young fellow and his girl from Plymouth. Roving the lanes a bit, you know. He's the son of a builder, and she's a receptionist in a café. We've been having a notice about the car every night on the wireless, and they've only just heard it, or only just decided to come forward. They corroborate the statement that Mrs Milne's car was pulled up to let them go over the bridge. But they didn't see anyone on the road. They're quite sure of it. They didn't know that bit of country, so those twists and turns and bridges took them by surprise, and he was driving with all his mind on them. So he says, anyway, and considering the cold weather, I dare say it's true.'

'And what was it that Riverfield told you?' said Toby.

'I reckon you've guessed it already. On the twenty-seventh of November, 1917, there was a marriage between Henry Rhymer and Anne Milton. Anne Milton was the daughter of the Reverend Edward Milton; she'd been born and bred in the parish. There was some sort of scandal about her, though whether it was Rhymer caused it or some other man, people don't seem sure now. She was twenty at the time, and here's her picture.' He tossed a photograph across to Toby.

With George looking over his shoulder, Toby examined it. It was a snapshot of a young woman in the uniform of the wartime VAD. She was pretty, yet less pretty, perhaps, than anyone, guessing at the youth of Anna Milne, might have expected. Without the grimness that marked it now, the grimness that, in a way, seemed to disfigure her face, it was oddly characterless. But without any question Anne Milton was Anna Milne; the strongly defined features, the dark, deep-set eyes, were the same, as well as something in the poise of that slimmer, lighter body.

Toby handed the photograph back to Whitear.

'And that makes her a murderess?' he asked.

Whitear gave him an amused look. 'It gives her a

motive for being one. Consider. Mrs Milne of The Laurels with her mink coat and her Bentley, her servants and her expensively educated and sheltered daughter—and Henry Rhymer, drink-sodden, down and out. Casting no aspersions on the state of matrimony, isn't there a motive in that?'

Toby was fiddling with a piece of twisted wire he had taken out of his pocket.

'Mrs Milne,' he remarked, 'is a woman of humane and kindly character.'

'Really?' said Whitear derisively. 'Is that so? If you ask around the place, Mr Dyke, you'll find she's got the name of being one of the toughest propositions they've had around here for a long time.'

Toby replied evenly: 'I asked around the place. When her gardener has toothache she pays for treatment and wants to buy him some false teeth. She doesn't mind if he swipes her whisky when he's feeling queer. When her cook's sister has too many children she tries to pay for her visit to a clinic. She doesn't get much gratitude, in fact her attempts at benevolence are probably thoroughly ill-judged, but the intention's above criticism. And she's able to win the liking and respect of that lonely, comic old woman up at Chovey Place.'

'You do it well, Mr Dyke—doesn't he, Eggbear?' said Whitear good-naturedly. 'But I can't believe you're wholly serious. Perhaps you'd like to come along with us now to The Laurels to watch over the good lady's interests, eh?' His violet eyes twinkled.

Eggbear suddenly leaned forward and took the piece of wire from Toby.

'What's this you got here?' he asked.

Toby tweaked it out of his hand and put it back in his pocket. 'When Whitear tells me what else he's got on Mrs Milne that's making him so pleased with himself,' he answered with a sour grin, 'perhaps I'll tell you.'

They covered the distance to The Laurels in the hired Sunbeam, the only car handy that would take the four of them. Both Toby and Eggbear were silent and thoughtful. Whitear, as usual, was gay and talkative, while George sat with his hands round his knees, keeping up a nervous, tuneless humming.

About halfway there, Eggbear asked Toby where he had found that piece of wire. Toby told him that it had risen, like a phoenix, out of the ashes. Eggbear frowned and turned to stare with dissatisfied eyes at the cottages they were passing.

Their arrival interrupted some of Daphne's desultory piano-playing. Her few remarks to them, while they waited for Mrs Milne, were disconnected, almost meaningless. She moved near to Toby, but this time it was not he that her eyes continually sought, but Whitear. His eyes were plainly contented to meet them.

Mrs Milne, with her usual composure and air of indifference, came in presently, but not until she had kept them waiting for several minutes. Her shrewd glance took in Whitear, and she seated herself so that she faced him directly.

He was obviously more impressed by her than he had expected, and while he hesitated for a moment, revising, perhaps, his first remark, Toby stole his opening.

'He's going to address you as Mrs Rhymer,' he said, 'and watch you flinch. Also, if he knows his duty, he's going to warn you that anything you say may be written down and used as evidence—'

'Mr Dyke!' said Whitear stormily.

Eggbear permitted himself a faint smile.

Mrs Milne, lighting a cigarette, remarked: 'I consider myself warned. Go ahead, Inspector.'

Muttering something peevishly to himself, Whitear tackled the job before him. 'Mrs Rhymer—I mean Mrs Milne—' He floundered, realizing his effect was not to be saved.

'Milne,' she said, 'is what I'm used to, but Rhymer is correct.'

At Toby's side Daphne gave a little gasp. It left her mouth hanging open with a childish look of horror. Her face had gone quite white.

Whitear ploughed on: 'You are Anne Milton, married to Henry Rhymer in 1917—'

'Yes, yes,' she said impatiently. 'It'll be quickest if you let me give you an account of the facts. Ever since I heard from Mr Dyke of the last anonymous letter he received I realized that sooner or later I should have to do that. If you'll just listen for a few minutes I can—'

'One moment, ma'am,' said Whitear. His handsome face was stern. 'At the inquest on the late Henry Rhymer you stated that you were unable to identify the corpse. You now admit that that evidence was false.'

'No, Inspector. At the time of the inquest I had an uncomfortable suspicion that the man I'd killed might be my own husband—what one might almost call a superstitious suspicion. For the only *fact* I possessed that suggested it to me was the fact that the man came from South Africa. Also, perhaps, the feeling that my luck couldn't last for ever, that sooner or later he'd turn up. But you wouldn't expect me to offer evidence as tenuous as that. When I looked at the body I definitely didn't recognize it. I hadn't seen my husband for about fifteen years. Of course, having just been told that this unknown man was from South Africa, and that he was drunk, the thought that he might be my husband was present in my mind. But I felt no certainty on the matter. And then no less a person than Sir Joseph Maxwell gave evidence that it was his son who'd been killed . . . No, I don't think I'll get into trouble over any of that, Inspector.'

Whitear looked at her quite unbelievingly.

Her ringed fingers flashed as she tapped her cigarette on the edge of an ash-tray. 'I know what you're going to say,' she said. 'You're going to point out that at the time of the inquest I already had in my possession the missing suitcase, and had even got as far as burning its contents before—'

'Mother!' Daphne interrupted shrilly. She was trembling violently.

Mrs Milne went straight on:—'before the inquest began, only, as it happens, there was nothing in that suitcase that pointed to the man being anyone but Shelley Maxwell.'

'Then why,' said Whitear swiftly, 'did you trouble to burn it?'

'I didn't burn the suitcase,' she replied. 'It's upstairs in my box-room. I only burned what was inside it—that's to say, a pair of flannel trousers, a toothbrush, a shaving-brush—the razor's in my dressing-table drawer—and a copy of an old newspaper. There were one or two handkerchiefs too, I think, and a shirt.'

'But why,' said Whitear, 'did you trouble to burn those things?'

'Because I didn't like the way they'd come into my possession. I thought there was something decidedly sinister about it.'

'Indeed? Having taken the cloakroom ticket from your husband's pocket as he lay by the roadside, you then sent your daughter—no, I beg your pardon, you sent some friend of yours first, to collect the suitcase from Wallaford and deposit it in Knightsteignton, then you sent your daughter to collect it from there, confusing the trail for us as far as you could. And you say there was something sinister in that. Well, I agree with you, ma'am, but—'

'But it wasn't like that!' Daphne broke in. 'It came by post, and it was my fault for going and getting it when mother said we'd better not do anything about it.'

Whitear turned to her. With a young, pretty, nervous girl before him, his sternness became more impressive.

'Would you mind repeating that more understandably, Miss Milne?' he said. '*It* came by post. The suitcase came by post?'

'No, no, the ticket. It came on Thursday morning. It was in an envelope addressed to mother—just the ticket and nothing else.'

'On *Thursday* morning?'

'Yes, on Thursday. I know it was. I'd just got back from London the evening before, and I hadn't seen mother at all because she was out to dinner. And when I came down to breakfast she was sitting there just opening the envelope. I noticed it because it was a funny-looking envelope; the address was done in block letters with a pencil. I asked what it was, and mother said she didn't know; she said it must be a joke or something. Then she showed me the ticket, and I said I'd go to Knightsteignton and see what it was, but she told me not to, and threw the thing into the wastepaper-basket. But I pulled it out afterwards and went off to Knightsteignton and got the suitcase. She was frightfully angry about it, and went straight off to Knightsteignton herself to ask who'd left the suitcase there. And she told me not to tell anyone—anyone at all—what had happened, and she burnt the things in the suitcase. Then next day the police came, and I thought it was about the suitcase, and I was simply terrified. But I didn't tell anyone, I didn't tell a soul, not even Adrian. I wanted to tell someone, terribly. I nearly told Mr Dyke, but I didn't!'

'I see,' said Whitear non-committally.

'It's true,' she said sharply, 'every word of it!'

'Just so. Now, Mrs Rhymer—' he turned back to the older woman, taking something from his pocket—'isn't this a copy of the same issue of the newspaper as the one you destroyed?'

She glanced at the paper he held out to her.

'Yes.'

'Is it in all respects the same?'

'The copy I destroyed,' she said, 'was a perfectly

ordinary copy, except that in one of the margins, against a report of a speech by Sir Joseph Maxwell, there was a comment in pencil: "The wise in heart will receive commandments, but the prating fool shall fall." I was completely puzzled by it, because I recognized the handwriting as Lady Maxwell's.'

Toby stretched out a hand. 'May I see?'

He took the paper as Whitear went on: 'Yet you thought it necessary to destroy that paper?'

While Mrs Milne was replying that, as she had already told him, the way in which the suitcase had been thrust upon her had made her exceedingly uneasy and she had therefore done her best to remove all traces of it, Toby unfolded the paper and glanced from page to page. It was a typical local daily, with columns devoted to a list of people who had sent floral tributes to a churchwarden's funeral, and more columns to those who had sent silver cruets to someone else's wedding. One whole page was occupied by a report and by photographs of some amateur theatricals. The play was a thriller called *The Return of Mr Chan*. Mr Chan, it appeared, was a suave and insinuating Chinese with a liking for inserting daggers with jewelled hilts between the shoulder-blades of public-school-educated *Britons*. Mr Chan had been acted by Adrian Laws. A photograph showed that only a little make-up had been necessary to turn his smooth, oval face into one quite presentably oriental. Daphne had acted the fair young girl whom a curly-haired young man, unknown to Toby, spent most of the three acts rescuing from Adrian's clutches. Major Maxwell had acted Daphne's father. Half-way down the page a photograph showed the head and shoulders of Mrs Milne. Beneath it the caption ran: 'Mrs Anna Milne, of The Laurels, Chovey, who produced the play.'

Toby looked up. Although she had been speaking to Whitear, her eyes, he found were on him.

He remarked: 'So this is once that the picture of Wendy

Bartlemy did get into the papers.'

'Yes—and look at all the trouble it's caused me.'

'It was, of course, by that picture,' said Whitear, 'that your husband traced you.'

'Yes. I'll tell you all about it if only you'll give me a chance. Daphne, you may as well stay and listen to this, unless you'd rather not.' Her voice was colourless, but her eyes on her daughter were filled with emotional defiance.

Daphne was tense. She said nothing, but she did not move.

Mrs Milne began: 'You've traced the fact that I came from Riverfield in Hampshire. My father was vicar there. During the war I worked as a VAD at a convalescent home in the neighbourhood. I was engaged to a man called Giles Wrothesley. I wanted to marry him when he came home on leave in the spring of nineteen-seventeen, but my parents wouldn't have it. I was only twenty. So we did the next best thing. About four months later he was killed.' She stubbed out her cigarette and lit a fresh one. 'Two months before Daphne was born I married Henry Rhymer. He was a South African—just a good-natured, easygoing being in a uniform, that was all I knew about him. And so far as it went it was correct; it was out of sheer kindness that he married me. I was desperately grateful. At that time there'd been no opportunity for his other qualities to show, his congenital dishonesty, his sottishness, the streak of sadism that came out whenever he found that a person despised him. I knew that he was weak, not very intelligent, in most ways a negligible kind of person. But that casually made gift of respectability to me and my daughter filled me with the belief that he was one of those "fine, simple, gallant souls whose kindness and gentleness count more than all the intelligence in the world"—you know the sort of idea. Wonderful what imagination can do! Daphne was born while he was back in France. As soon as I was able I went to London and got a job. When Henry came back I kept him. I was proud to be able to do it. Then I was less proud but still dutiful . . .'

Her harsh voice hesitated. It was as if, for a moment, she were wondering whether to let herself go, to let out of herself some of the old misery and anger. But with her brooding eyes on Daphne she went on with her story, keeping it bare of all detail.

'After about a year we went to South Africa. Henry said he'd never get on in England. I was glad to go and escape from creditors and charitable friends, uncomfortable memories and all the rest of it. Unfortunately those accumulated in South Africa even faster than at home. After another eighteen months I left him. And then—' she gave a laugh—'then the chase began. My idea was to save up enough money to get back to England without him, but wherever I went he followed, and with pathos and threats got the money out of me. At first I didn't actually hide from him. But I took to it quite soon, only he was amazingly cunning at finding me. Have I mentioned the streak of almost mad, deliberate cruelty in him? It showed only now and then, two or three times in the years I knew him, but . . . Anyway, I got enough money together at last to get back to England with Daphne. I know you remember that voyage, Daphne, though not much that went before. I know you don't remember Henry Rhymer. I'd already started creating for you the picture of Tony Milne—who wasn't quite an invention, but was very like Giles. We got to England and—'

'But,' said Daphne suddenly, coming out of her tense stupor with a flinging up of her head and a blazing of blood in her cheeks, '—*but I was born in nineteen seventeen*!'

Her mother nodded. 'Henry had let some friends of his in South Africa know the date of his marriage. So we decided, when we went over, that we'd take a year off your age. You were small and babyish-looking; no one thought there was anything queer about it.'

'But,' said Daphne, her voice high and strained, 'when my birthday comes next week I'll be twenty-one, not twenty!'

'Yes, that's quite true.'

'And you've been letting me think I was twenty, and telling me I wouldn't be able to marry Adrian till I was twenty-one. You've been playing a trick on me!'

'Daphne—'

'You have, you've played a trick on me! And after what your own parents did to you. I'll never forgive you. It's so mean and—and—it's *so mean*!'

'But, Daphne, it's quite, oh, it's quite different. Giles wasn't like . . .'

'Oh yes, my father was the man *you* loved, while Adrian's only the one *I* love. I know you hate him, but you can't do anything about it now. I'll marry him next week. I'll marry him the very day after my birthday—'

'Ahem.' It was Inspector Whitear. 'If you wouldn't mind, Miss Milne, allowing your mother to continue . . .'

By no expression on her face did it show that Daphne had heard, yet, as if the set features of her mother were more than she could bear to look at, she made a dive out of the room. Anna Milne let a slow breath escape her. Her skin had a white and withered look; the deep tone of the lipstick on her tightly closed lips seemed almost purple against it.

She turned her head to Whitear. 'It's fifteen years since I got back to England. I worked at one thing and another, then I had a little luck with journalism, some short stories and things. Then I tried my hand at a novel. I thought it was the most wonderful thing in the world when I got fifty pounds for it. I called myself Wendy Bartlemy. I've been successful—that's to say, I've made money and I've made myself a not too reputable name. But I never let a photograph of myself get into any newspaper, I never granted an interview. Fear's a thing that dies hard

—never dies, sometimes. If I left the faintest trail behind me, Rhymer, I was sure, would pick it up. Sometimes, after ten years, twelve years, I said to myself that I'd lost all rationality, and that there couldn't be the slightest harm in letting myself be known. But something always checked me. And at last, after fifteen years, he found me . . .'

Whitear shifted his chair a little. Eggbear, who had been frowning at the floor, cleared his throat. Toby folded up the newspaper he was still holding into neat folds. George sat still, regarding himself from across the room in the convex mirror over the fireplace, as if he could never grow tired of the shape it made of his face.

Toby rose to his feet.

'And now,' he said to Whitear, 'you've got your motive all nice and plain. Opportunity, motive, and three anonymous letters. What else have you got?'

'This,' said Whitear, and took from his pocket, wrapped in a cloth, the whisky flask that George had looked for vainly that morning.

CHAPTER 14

'Let me explain,' said Whitear.

He rose and splayed his feet on the hearth-rug. He exuded quiet dignity.

'Rhymer,' he said, 'was drunk when he died.'

No one questioned it.

'Very well,' said Whitear. 'He was drunk. But not only was he drunk; he had drunk whisky a very few minutes before he was killed.'

He looked round at them all again. Mrs Milne gave a nod, but something about it suggested that she had no idea what he had said and had nodded merely out of automatic politeness.

As he continued, however, she made an effort to bring her attention back to him.

'We all know,' said Whitear, 'that this flask—' he held it up—'has been suggested as the possible container of the whisky. We've found no other container. We all know that if it was the container, then the whisky must have been given to Rhymer by Mrs Milne herself. Now, Mrs Milne maintains that she did not handle the flask since the time of the big accident last December, except to refill it on the evening of the same day. According to her gardener, however, it was half full on Tuesday, the day of the accident that concerns us, yet on the Friday—' Again he peered round at them all. Toby muttered impatiently. 'On the Friday it was empty! A curious flask. It empties itself, one must suppose, by evaporation through a closed stopper. Decidedly curious. And yet, you'll be interested to know, that isn't its most curious habit. This is a flask that polishes itself.'

Toby was derisive. 'If you mean there are no fingerprints—'

But Whitear raised his hand. 'There *are* fingerprints. There are your own—and those of your friend—er—George, and Eggbear's. When you were looking at the flask yourselves it was handed round from one to the other, I believe. Very clear prints they are too, on a fine polished surface. The gardener's also appear, a finger and thumb, a bit smudged, just below the stopper. He says he handled it gingerly because his hands had earth on them. He also verifies what the maid says—the one who refilled the flask for him. She says she was cleaning the silver at the time, and had on a pair of gloves. That explains why her prints do not appear. She's certain too that she didn't give the flask a wipe over. Now—' He made another of his effective pauses; his voice, when he continued, was very gentle. 'Now can anyone explain to me why that flask had none of Mrs Milne's fingerprints on it?'

She gave a start. Her cigarette sprayed ash on to the carpet. Yet it was more as if it had been the mere mention of her own name, jerking her mind back to what was happening, rather than the question itself, that had contained the shock. All the time Whitear had been speaking she had kept glancing towards the door as if she thought Daphne might reappear at any moment. Her face had the absentmindedness of brooding passion.

No one answered the question. One of Toby's hands was caressing his long chin.

Whitear said softly: 'Who polished the flask?'

He waited. He added: 'And why?'

In the convex mirror on the wall the room and the people in it had the look of a carefully composed picture.

'Who was it,' said Whitear, 'who removed from the flask the prints that Mrs Milne must have made when she handled it at the time of the December accident, and when she was refilling it afterwards? Very likely they would not have been clearly identifiable, but who, in that case, removed the blurred impressions? Who polished it some time between Tuesday and Friday—because if the polishing had been done earlier than the Tuesday the gardener's prints would have shown on it again. It was only on the Friday that he gripped it so delicately by the neck.'

'I know you're going to say that it was I,' said Mrs Milne wearily, 'but why should I remove my fingerprints from my own flask?'

He turned on her swiftly. 'Because,' he said, 'there were other fingerprints as well—the fingerprints of Henry Rhymer.'

Toby swung himself up from his chair. He stood there stretching. 'And I thought,' he said, 'that perhaps you'd really got somewhere. Listen, Whitear, I'll tell you a few things you ought to know. The first is that Mrs Milne is not a crackbrained idiot. She's a fool, and in some ways she's nervously unbalanced, but I've noticed no signs of mental deficiency.'

She murmured words of thanks.

'Go ahead,' said Whitear.

'Have you tried imagining this thing that you think took place?' said Toby. 'Have you made a picture of it in your mind and tried to *see* what must have happened? Let me touch it in a bit for you. She sees the man Rhymer ahead of her, she stops her car, gets out and talks to him—that's your idea, isn't it?—and gives him a drink from her flask. He's so tight it's easy for her to push him over and then drive her car over his head. OK. Then she remembers her flask. Rhymer held it while he drank; it's got his fingerprints on it. So she takes it out of the pigeon-hole on the dash and polishes it up. OK. But, Whitear, since it's her own flask, will she be careful to handle it so that her own prints don't reappear? Will she hold it with her handkerchief? Will she do the job wearing those heavy, fingerless, fur-backed driving-gloves you probably found in the pigeon-hole, when it'd be so much easier to slip her hand out? If there were any reason to conceal her fingerprints it'd be worth the trouble, but there isn't one. That's why I made the remarks about her sanity; she'd know there weren't any reasons. She's a quick-thinking, practical woman; she might make mistakes, but not mistakes of that kind. She'd hold the flask naturally in her hand, polish it up and put it back; her own marks'd be all over it. No, Whitear, if you want the person who polished it up you've got to look somewhere else. If you want the person who emptied it you've got to look somewhere else. If you want the person who murdered Henry Rhymer you've got to look somewhere else!'

Whitear's face was set but his voice had its usual politeness. 'Indeed? And where is that, Mr Dyke?'

'If you'll come for a little ride in my car, I'll show you.'

Eggbear's head jerked up from his still frowning contemplation of the carpet.

'Coming?' said Toby.

Suddenly indecisive, Whitear's gaze escaped from Toby's, only to meet the strained, sharp gaze of Mrs Milne. Quickly his eyes shifted from meeting her intensity. Eggbear made a movement towards the door. The sergeant said nothing, yet his reliance on Toby was so apparent that it affected Whitear like a puff of wind swelling a sagging sail. He shrugged his shoulders and said something vague, but he took a step towards the door. Triumph gleamed on Toby's face. He looked past Whitear to Mrs Milne, and, very faintly, she smiled.

But on that ravaged face a smile was curiously dreadful.

Outside, the four men took their places in the old Sunbeam. Before starting, however, Toby got out of the car and ran into the house once more. He was gone only two or three minutes. Returning and starting the car, he steered them on to the familiar road to Purbrook. Whitear sat beside him, Eggbear and George behind. Toby and George irritated Whitear by insisting on singing to themselves as they drove along, and singing different tunes. Eggbear sniffed at the darkness and said that a thaw was coming.

'And if it do, us'll be pickin' violets for a pastime; the bed's just a mist o' buds,' he told them. 'Needs only a spot o' warm to bring'n on.'

The lights of the car picked out bare hedges, a labourer and a dog, the corpse of a rabbit in the middle of the road. With its slow dignity the car lumbered along. Twice the lights flickered and went out, and Toby had to stop his song to tell George to get down and see to them. Whitear fidgeted but contained his impatience and curiosity.

At length, beyond Purbrook, they came to the grey stone cottage, 'the converted cow-house, rapidly reverting to its original beliefs,' as Adrian Laws had called it. Beside the lonely road, with the silence of the moor pressing upon it, and the darkness swallowing it again the moment the lights of the car had slid across its face, it was desolate as the dream of a fear-ridden mind. Eggbear muttered that he didn't know how a young chap could live there all alone.

With Eggbear's torch showing them the neglected path, they hurried up to the door. Toby did not knock, and the door, unlocked as the doors of country cottages often are, yielded at once as he thrust his hand at the latch. Dim light met them, the dim light of an oil lamp, turned low, alight in the sitting-room. The sitting-room door stood wide open.

They stood there, the four of them grouped silently in the small, dark kitchen, staring at what was before them. Then Whitear strode through, to look down into the dead face of the young man, lolling in his big armchair, and to stoop and pick up from the floor the revolver that had slipped from the limp hand.

Eggbear, breathing hard, looked round at Toby.

'What was it you told'n, Toby, when you telephoned, back to The Laurels?'

'Did you see me telephoning?' said Toby.

'No, but I allow that's what you done when you went back into the house.'

After an instant's pause and preparing to follow Whitear, Toby replied: 'All I told him was that I'd found a piece of twisted wire.'

'—And if he hadn't killed himself,' said Toby, later that evening, 'we might never have been able to do anything about it. We could have brought the anonymous letters home to him all right, but we'd probably have had to let the murder roost.'

'Which only goes to prove—'

But Toby snatched the words out of Whitear's mouth: '—that everyone makes a mistake some time. The proof of the platitude is in the eating. Only suicide is rather a final sort of mistake, isn't it? His trouble was that he never tried to think the business out whole. He was an opportunist; he merely made use of whatever happened to turn up. So he wasn't clear about what he'd let himself in for, lost his head, and . . .'

'Maybe,' said Eggbear, ''twas his conscience he couldn't face, or the thought of his girl knowin'.'

'Oh yes, he probably hadn't quite outgrown a conscience, and certainly he hadn't outgrown his vanity. But he lost his head, too, when he realized just how big a blunder he'd made—he must have. If he'd given himself time to think, he'd have been able to argue conscience and vanity into backing him up as usual. He was pretty good at that.'

'Just which blunder,' said Whitear slowly, frowning at the ground, 'are you referring to?'

'The last of the letters, of course,' said Toby.

'But it gave us what we needed against Mrs Milne.'

'And if you think it out,' said Toby, 'what blunder could have been bigger than that? It was a bigger blunder even than the typography. Look here, I'll run over it, and you'll see what I mean. What was the first fishy thing about this whole case?'

It was Eggbear who answered promptly: 'The missing bottle.'

'No,' said Toby.

'But—'

'We-ell, perhaps it was the first thing you could have got on to. But the first fishy thing, if you could have spotted it—and you *should* have spotted it as soon as you heard from that landlady in Wallaford—was the piece of paper in the dead man's pocket, the paper that had Mrs Milne's name and address on it. Think it out. What did that paper make you think? It made you believe that the man was on his way to visit Mrs Milne. Now if he had come from South Africa with the name and address of someone he intended visiting in England, the paper on which that name and address were written down would be an important paper, wouldn't it? A paper to be preserved with the utmost care.'

'Well, he did preserve it,' said Whitear.

'But a traveller has other important papers, hasn't he? A passport, for instance. But Rhymer's passport—the Maxwell passport, that's to say, which he was using as his own—was left behind in Wallaford.'

'You mean,' said Whitear, 'that if he'd forgotten the one he'd have forgotten the other?'

Toby nodded. 'You can't see him carefully separating them out when he decided to change his suit, can you? You can't see him getting up in the morning, deciding to put on the more or less clean suit he'd got in his bag, going to the coat he's put on a hanger the night before, and taking out this paper with the address, but leaving everything else behind—particularly as he seems to have used his passport as a sort of pocket-book. No, he'd have taken the lot or forgotten the lot. Or so it seemed to me. That paper breathed to me a rich and promising fishiness. It meant, d'you see, that either he'd met someone who'd given him the address which he'd written down on an odd scrap of paper in his pocket, or—and this was of course the more entertaining thought—someone had seen fit to plant it on him. But in either case there was someone—someone he'd met and talked to after leaving Mrs Quantick's lodging-house. Not that any of this could be proved. It was some time before Laws let us have an actual proof that he'd met and spoken to Rhymer. But from the first I was certain that there'd been someone with whom Rhymer had spent the hour or two before his death, someone who'd got him as generally tight as he was, and then given him that final drink we knew he must have had just before he was killed. For Rhymer must have got his drink from somewhere, and we knew it wasn't from any of the pubs for miles around, and he must have done something with the bottle the last drink came out of.'

'The flask in the car—' Whitear began.

'I'm coming to the flask. But in any case, it could only have accounted for the last drink, not for all the others. Now let's shift to the first anonymous letter.'

'It started us thinkin' about the flask,' said Eggbear.

'Yes, but it started us thinking about who'd written it, too, and why they'd written it. But it was a clever letter. Of course it might have come from someone who'd actually seen Mrs Milne give Rhymer the drink, but it could also have come from anyone who knew no more than the facts made public at the inquest, plus the fact that Mrs Milne was in the habit of keeping a flask in her car. It could have been a guess, following a little shrewd deduction; there was nothing in it to prove that the writer *knew* anything. As for why it'd been written, it might have been an attempt to lead us to the truth by someone who didn't want to get involved in giving evidence, it might have been an attempt to frame Mrs Milne, or it might have been generalized spite. Mrs Milne seems to be pretty thoroughly disliked in certain quarters; spite was quite a plausible explanation. But spite—' and Toby shifted his position on his hard chair—'spite wasn't a very interesting explanation. I liked both the others much better. I liked the idea that either she'd done a murder or was being framed for one. So on that assumption I went ahead, accepting, of course, the implication that the letter-writer possessed real knowledge of what had happened, even if I couldn't prove that he did. Someone who knew, someone who had seen the death of Rhymer, someone who had filled Rhymer up with whisky, someone who picked up Rhymer's suitcase from Wallaford, someone who wanted to land Mrs Milne in the worst trouble the law can make, someone . . . well, someone was taking shape, you'll agree, someone was quite concrete enough to keep me interested in this neighbourhood.'

'Yes, but why should you decide,' said Whitear fretfully, 'that that person had gone and done Rhymer in himself? What motive had he?'

'I didn't decide that he had,' said Toby, 'till I saw Adrian dead. I thought it probable, that's all. I wasn't convinced that Mrs Milne hadn't done the murder until I learnt that the flask had none of her fingerprints on it. Then I knew that the flask was part of the frame-up. You see, when Laws thought what it'd look like if he suggested to us that it was Mrs Milne who'd given Rhymer the whisky, he naturally took care that the flask should be emptied. He slipped into the garage some time on Thursday evening, I expect, and poured the whisky away. But it was only when he'd done it that it occurred to him he ought to have worn gloves for the job. He put it right as well as he could by giving the flask a polish, but that removed, of course, the fingerprints of Mrs Milne, which, as I explained before, she'd never have removed herself. I was very grateful to you for doing that bit of work on the flask, Whitear. As for motive—' Toby gave a wave of his hand, as if indicating a tropical luxuriance of motives—'as soon as one got to know a bit about the relationships among that group of people, Laws, the Milnes and the Maxwells, the motive glared at one. Laws wanted to marry Daphne Milne. He was staying on here, leading a life he'd found disappointing and dull, in the hope that he could marry her. How much he wanted the girl herself it's no use our guessing; that he wanted her money we can be pretty sure. He hated his poverty. He hated it with malice and envy. Not that Daphne's got any money that I know of, but her mother's got a lot, and some day it'll all be Daphne's. If the mother could be got rid of . . .'

'But do you mean to say,' said Eggbear, 'that that young fellow was plannin', right from the moment he run across Rhymer, to bring Mrs Milne to the gallows?'

'No, he did very little planning,' said Toby. 'I told you, he was an opportunist. I think he killed Rhymer because he saw him as a competitive claim on the Milne fortune. He'd have been rather an undesirable father-in-law too, wouldn't he? I should think Laws' ideas were pretty vague when he decided on Mrs Milne's car as the one to shove Rhymer down in front of. He couldn't have thought over the bottle-letter yet, because he didn't know that you chaps were going to start worrying about that straight away. All along he made use of other people's actions rather than planning his own ahead. This is how I see him going about it; on Tuesday evening, a little after half-past six, he turned up at The Laurels in answer to a note Mrs Milne had left at his cottage, asking him to look in on her. I know he said he never got that note, and that he never came, but the two servants at The Laurels heard his car arrive, stop for a bit, then go away again. Well, I think it was when he stopped that he first met Rhymer. He and Rhymer probably arrived at the gate at the same time, and Rhymer very likely asked him if this was where Mrs Milne lived. Adrian was always interested in other people's affairs; he'd have got Rhymer talking, and then suggested that they should go out to Adrian's place. He could have pointed out that Mrs Milne had certainly gone off to her badminton club by then and wouldn't be home again until pretty well midnight. At the cottage he filled Rhymer up with whisky, and very likely got out of him the whole story of Maxwell, as well as the truth about Mrs Milne. Then he took Rhymer along in his car, which he probably left inside one of the field gates along the road, to the spot with the two bridges. He took a flask with him. Then, when he recognized the Bentley, he gave Rhymer a wallop on the head and sent him spinning into the road. He stayed behind the hedge himself until Mrs Milne went off for the police, then he came out and planted the paper with her name and address on it in Rhymer's pocket—'

'And,' said Eggbear, 'found the ticket for the suitcase.'

'That's right,' said Toby. 'He went off to Wallaford next day, and to pick up the suitcase thoughtfully put on the wig he'd worn as the Chinese murderer in some theatricals here a few months ago—a sleek, black wig; you've seen the photograph. He got the suitcase, took a look inside it, and decided to plant it on Mrs Milne. So he deposited it at Knightsteignton and sent her the ticket. Daphne picked it up—you know that bit of it. That evening he ran across me in the Ring of Bells, and decided to use me in elucidating the puzzle in the way he wanted.'

'And that,' said George, 'is where he made his biggest mistake of all—eh, Tobe?'

Tobe nodded gravely. 'Yes, his attempts to lead me by the nose were a touch too crude. That's how I first got thinking about him. When I went up to the Milnes, asking if they'd take me to the Maxwells, it was he who offered to do it, after Mrs Milne had definitely refused. Then, when we got there, it was he who arranged how I was to approach Lady Maxwell. He didn't know why I wanted to go there, but he took good care that I should hear all her reasons for insisting that the dead man wasn't her son. Again, why? So I started giving some attention to Laws. He seemed to have it in common with the writer of the letter that he wanted to help me to find out—well, at least a certain amount. And I recognized his motive. Major Maxwell, to whom I gave a certain amount of thought, had a motive for killing Rhymer, since he wanted to marry his wife, but none that I could see for involving Mrs Milne herself in trouble. But Laws had a motive that cut in both directions. The only other serious suspect was Mrs Milne herself—seriously suspected by the major as well as by you, Whitear, and now and then by me. Even so, there was that letter-writer hanging around and needing smelling out. So I concentrated on him, and let the murder take care of itself.'

'As it did,' said Whitear.

'We-ell,' said Eggbear, 'you got to remember that telephone call of Toby's. Not quite, it didn't take care of itself.'

'I'm coming to that,' said Toby. 'Laws didn't think we were getting on fast enough, so he sent me the second anonymous letter. Like the first, it contained nothing that proved that the writer had ever met Rhymer. We all knew about the coat that had been left at Mrs Quantick's, and that the suitcase was missing, and the whole village could have known that Mrs Milne was making a bonfire on Thursday afternoon. Anyone with a nasty mind could have put the three facts together. But when we get to the third letter—yet, come to think of it, Laws made a mistake even with the second. An odd little one. It wasn't in the letter itself, it was up at the Maxwells, when I got Mrs Milne to go there to show them the letter. They were all there, old Maxwell and his wife, the major and Laws. Major Maxwell gave the letter to Sir Joseph; Lady Maxwell wanted a look at it and it was handed over to her; Major Maxwell took it from her and examined it. But Adrian—inquisitive, interested Adrian—never touched the thing. He looked at it, but only from a distance. I know it's nothing much to go on, but because it struck me as thoroughly unnatural—after all, one always wants to get one's hands on a thing like that—I stored it up and went on considering the case of Adrian Laws with more curiosity than ever. And then came letter number three . . .'

Toby interrupted himself to give a sudden, wide yawn in the faces of his listeners. 'Late, isn't it, Sam—or is it just that I've been getting up too early? Well, that third letter couldn't have been written by anyone who hadn't had a good talk with Rhymer. The information in it couldn't have been deduced from the surrounding circumstances. You can't deduce the dates and places of marriages from surrounding circumstances. Rhymer had *told* Laws where and when he and Anne Milton were married. And he hadn't told him a thing of that kind inside two or three minutes' conversation somewhere on the road; he'd taken quite a while to get round to the subject, and probably quite a few drinks. From the time I got that letter I knew that the letter-writer was the person who had been with Rhymer up to the time of his death . . . and it was from that same letter that I also became certain that Laws was the letter-writer. I'll explain: Both of the other letters were put together with letters clipped out of ordinary daily papers; so was this one, except for the one word 'November'. That was in an odd sort of type; only a very precious kind of production would use it. Well, when I was out visiting Laws—I wanted to ask him what he'd been doing on the Wednesday morning after the accident, in case he'd any sort of an alibi for the time I believed he'd been picking up and getting rid of the suitcase, and, as a matter of fact, he hadn't—'

'Nor'd Major Maxwell,' Eggbear put in. 'He spent the morning in bed with a notice on his door tellin' Mrs Deller, who does for him, that he didn't want to be waked. He told me he'd been sleepin' badly and didn't want to be roused in case he did manage to doze off for a bit.'

'Yes, you see, the tall, dark man with the glasses arrived at Knightsteignton by train, not car. The major's car was out of order. But though Laws had got a car, it's such a distinctive one that he'd never go in it if he was engaged on any shady business. Well, as I was saying, when I was out at the cottage I came on a fancy little monthly called *New Voices*, printed in the type I was looking for, and bound with a pretty spiral wire. And the November number was missing. And a spiral wire was in the top layer of ashes in his ash-bin, where the remnants of that November number were too, I expect, only not in a recognizable condition. He must have been in an awful hurry to catch the post to go and use a whole word of a type as noticeable as that, or he must have been losing his nerve already or something . . .' Again Toby yawned, and asked Eggbear how late it was, because, he said, there was some writing he wanted to do before he went to bed.

But Eggbear only prompted him: 'And what revolver, Toby? How'd he get hold of that?'

'Oh, it was Major Maxwell's,' said Toby. 'When I left he probably realized that he'd not much chance of coming through. So he borrowed it while the major was picking up seed catalogues in Wallaford.'

'But look here, Dyke,' said Whitear, 'that call you put through to him from The Laurels—what the devil d'you think you were up to, doing a thing like that? You were warning him. It was a gross interference with the course of the law!'

'My dear man,' said Toby wearily, 'the law got him. The law of his own nature. There's no other that could have touched him.'

'And so, Mr Poppenheimer,' said Mrs Milne, meeting George in the road near her home a couple of days later, 'your friend has done quite nicely out of the newspapers after all.'

George was scrambling out of the ditch where he had discovered a couple of primroses. The thaw, as Sergeant Eggbear had prophesied, had come; the sergeant's garden was fragrant with huge violets. In the ditches, too, a few primroses were hurrying to greet the West Country warmth.

George stood pinning the two he had found into the side of his cap.

'That's so,' he said.

'And the fee he asked me was hardly—small,' said Mrs Milne.

'Oh, well, it's always nice when you make something out of a holiday,' said George, 'ain't it?' He set the cap, gay as the promise of spring, on the side of his head. 'And at least he found out who was writing those letters, just like you wanted.'

'Oh, I'm grateful,' she answered.

'So you ought to be,' said George, 'because, mind you,

if Toby was a bit different . . .'

When he paused she asked him: 'What d'you mean?'

'Well, ma'am,' said George, turning and walking beside her towards her gate, 'I've known Toby a long time. He's one of the best chaps in the world. I'd back him in anything—that didn't involve judgment.'

She laughed. 'But I don't understand. He's a very intelligent, really quite a brilliant man. It's lucky for me that he is.'

'It's lucky for you,' said George, 'that he's just as brilliant and intelligent as he is, and not a ha'porth more. But take it from me, he follows that big nose of his a lot too fast. Now take the matter of the third letter and the blunder in it—'

'He told me all about that,' she said quickly. 'I saw the point. It really was a very bad blunder of Adrian's, letting it appear that he'd talked to Henry.'

'A blunder?' said George. 'I should say it *was* a blunder. Such a blunder that I says to myself: would a cute young chap like Laws ever make a mistake of that kind? Then I says to myself: and who benefits by this so-called blunder of his, eh? And I answers: our Mrs Milne. Because even if it gives away that she's Mrs Rhymer, she's slick enough to know we're going to find that out anyway. Then I says: and who was it grinned all over her face when young Laws wouldn't back up her story about his being the man she was expecting? And I answers: Mrs Milne, and I reckon she was grinning because she was glad to know for certain sure at last it was Laws who was trying to do her down. He gave himself away, you see, when he wouldn't back up her perfectly true story. And who's clever enough to use that bit of fancy type to make us sure the letter was from young Laws, and to throw that wire into the top layer of ashes where we'd be sure to find it? And again the answer is—'

'Mrs Milne. So I wrote that letter about myself, did I?'

They had reached the gate. Each was leaning an elbow upon it.

'Certain sure you wrote it,' said George. 'Who else would ever have thought of such a thing?'

'Really? And—er—did I murder my husband, if you don't mind my asking?'

'Murder?' said George. 'That wasn't any murder. It was an accident—couldn't have been anything else. See here, you know what that bit of road's like. And you know that the couple in the sports car didn't see a thing. When they come past there wasn't a soul in the road. So Rhymer and young Laws must've been behind the hedge, mustn't they? But it was in the middle between the two bridges you went over Rhymer, and you can't hide behind the hedge there; for one thing, it isn't a hedge, it's a fence, and it drops down straight into those meadows the other side of it. They'd have had to be beyond the second bridge, and that means Laws'd have had to follow Rhymer over it and knock him down, or knock him down and carry him over it. But if he'd done that you'd have seen him yourself. No, he must just've let Rhymer loose in the road, and Rhymer went hareing over the bridge on his own and fell down and you did him in, innocent and accidental, like you said. O' course, you might call it homicidal to let a bloke as tight as that loose in a road with a car just coming, but I reckon all Laws really wanted was a chance to listen in to the fun when you and your husband met. He couldn't've done it if he let you meet at home. The only murder he ever tried to commit was when he tried to get you jerking at the end of a rope. That was his real murder, not the other—and nasty enough, if you ask me, to deserve getting shot.'

She was watching his face detachedly. 'But if you're right, and I'd be glad to think you were, why did Adrian shoot himself? It looked, it's been accepted, as a complete confession of guilt.'

He gave a lop-sided grin. 'Yes, and who's clever enough, I'd like to know, to think that it would be? And who knew the police were going out to the cottage with more than half an idea in their minds that it was a murderer they were calling on? Who heard Toby tip the so-called murderer off that he was caught—so that Toby himself wasn't going to be at all surprised at a suicide? Who'd snitched a revolver that morning in case she got into such bad trouble it might be worth having handy? Who's got a Bentley that could get round by the other road to Purbrook, even if it's a bit longer that way, in half the time the old Sunbeam could make it in? Who's got a daughter she loves near to craziness, who swears she's going to marry the man who's been trying to land her mother on the gallows? *Who doesn't mind taking long chances?*'

There was a silence. From the short, brown catkins in the hedges, drops of moisture splashed down upon the grass of the verge.

'You've absolutely no proof of any of this,' said Anna Milne.

'And that clears the air a whole lot, don't it?' said George. 'But you know, Tobe was right about one thing, anyway. He kept saying that girl was in it somewhere. So she was, the poor kid, bang in the middle of it.'

He raised his flowered cap. But just as he was starting down the road towards Chovey he hesitated before her. 'You know,' he said, 'Tobe's got a quick sort of brain and lots of imagination, and that's how he takes himself in. Because it don't occur to him, see, that anyone could expect what he's expecting until he starts expecting them to expect it. What I mean is—'

'Yes, yes,' she said, 'I see. Goodbye, Mr Pinkerton.'

'Prendergast,' he corrected her, and set off down the road.